Wintergirls

wintergirls

LAURIE HALSE ANDERSON

Viking

Viking

Published by Penguin Group

Penguin Group (USA) Inc., 345 Hudson Street, New York, New York 10014, U.S.A.

Penguin Group (Canada), 90 Eglinton Avenue East, Suite 700, Toronto,

Ontario, Canada M4P 2Y3 (a division of Pearson Penguin Canada Inc.)

Penguin Books Ltd, Registered Offices: 80 Strand, London WC2R 0RL, England

First published in 2009 by Viking, a member of Penguin Group (USA) Inc.

3 5 7 9 10 8 6 4

LIBRARY OF CONGRESS CATALOGING-IN-PUBLICATION DATA

Anderson, Laurie Halse.

Wintergirls / by Laurie Halse Anderson.

p. cm.

Summary: Eighteen-year-old Lia comes to terms with her best friend's death from anorexia as she

struggles with the same disorder.

ISBN 978-0-670-01110-0 (hardcover)

[1. Anorexia nervosa—Fiction. 2. Death—Fiction.] I. Title.

PZ7.A54385Wi 2009

[Fic]—dc22

2008037452

To Scot—for building the fire that keeps me warm when the blizzard rages outside.

[Persephone] was filled with a sense of wonder, and she reached out with both hands to take hold of the pretty plaything. And the earth, full of roads leading every which way, opened up under her. . . . She cried with a piercing voice. . . . But not one of the immortal ones, or of human mortals, heard her.

Homeric Hymn to Demeter, translated by Gregory Nagy

The King gave orders that they should let her sleep quietly till the time came for her to awake.

The Sleeping Beauty in the Woods, by Charles Perrault, 1696, translated by Charles Welsh

So she tells me, the words dribbling out with the cranberry muffin crumbs, commas dunked in her coffee.

She tells me in four sentences. No, five.

I can't let me hear this, but it's too late. The facts
sneak in and stab me. When she gets to the worst part

           . . . body found in a motel room, alone . . .

. . . my walls go up and my doors lock. I nod like I'm listening, like we're communicating, and she never knows the
difference.

    It's not nice when girls die.

"We didn't want you hearing it at school or on the news."
Jennifer crams the last hunk of muffin into her mouth.
"Are you sure you're okay?"

I open the dishwasher and lean into the cloud of steam

that floats out of it. I wish I could crawl in and curl up between a bowl and a plate. ~~My stepmother~~ Jennifer could lock the door, twist the dial to SCALD, and press ON.

The steam freezes when it touches my face. "I'm fine," I lie.

She reaches for the box of oatmeal raisin cookies on the table. "This must feel awful." She rips off the cardboard ribbon. "Worse than awful. Can you get me a clean container?"

I take a clear plastic box and lid out of the cupboard and hand it across the island to her. "Where's Dad?"

"He had a tenure meeting."

"Who told you about Cassie?"

She crumbles the edges of the cookies before she puts them in the box, to make it look like she baked instead of bought. "Your mother called late last night with the news. She wants you to see Dr. Parker right away instead of waiting for your next appointment."

"What do you think?" I ask.

"It's a good idea," she says. "I'll see if she can fit you in this afternoon."

"Don't bother." I pull out the top rack of the dishwasher. The glasses vibrate with little screams when I touch them. If I pick them up, they'll shatter. "There's no point."

She pauses in mid-crumble. "Cassie was your best friend."

"Not anymore. I'll see Dr. Parker next week like I'm supposed to."

"I guess it's your decision. Will you promise me you'll call your mom and talk to her about it?"

"Promise."

Jennifer looks at the clock on the microwave and shouts, "Emma—four minutes!"

~~My stepsister~~ Emma doesn't answer. She's in the family room, hypnotized by the television and a bowl of blue cereal.

Jennifer nibbles a cookie. "I hate to speak ill of the dead, but I'm glad you didn't hang out with her anymore."

I push the top rack back in and pull out the bottom. "Why?"

"Cassie was a mess. She could have taken you down with her."

I reach for the steak knife hiding in the nest of spoons. The black handle is warm. As I pull it free, the blade slices the air, dividing the kitchen into slivers. There is Jennifer, packing store-bought cookies in a plastic tub for her daughter's class. There is Dad's empty chair, pretending he has no choice about these early meetings. There is the shadow of my mother, who prefers the phone because face-to-face takes too much time and usually ends in screaming.

Here stands a girl clutching a knife. There is grease on the stove, blood in the air, and angry words piled in the corners. We are trained not to see it, not to see any of it.

. . . body found in a motel room, alone . . .

Someone just ripped off my eyelids.

"Thank God you're stronger than she was." Jennifer drains her coffee mug and wipes the crumbs from the corners of her mouth.

The knife slides into the butcher block with a whisper. "Yeah." I reach for a plate, scrubbed free of blood and gristle. It weighs ten pounds.

She snaps the lid on the box of cookies. "I have a late settlement appointment. Can you take Emma to soccer? Practice starts at five."

"Which field?"

"Richland Park, out past the mall. Here." She hands the heavy mug to me, her lipstick a bloody crescent on the rim. I set it on the counter and unload the plates one at a time, arms shaking.

Emma comes into the kitchen and sets her cereal bowl, half-filled with sky-colored milk, next to the sink.

"Did you remember the cookies?" she asks her mother.

Jennifer shakes the plastic container. "We're late, honey. Get your stuff."

Emma trudges toward her backpack, her sneaker laces flopping. She should still be sleeping, but my father's wife drives her to school early four mornings a week for violin lessons and conversational French. Third grade is not too young for enrichment, you know.

Jennifer stands up. The fabric of her skirt is pulled so tight over her thighs, the pockets gape open. She tries to smooth out the wrinkles. "Don't let Emma con you into buying chips before practice. If she's hungry, she can have a fruit cup."

"Should I stick around and drive her home?"

She shakes her head. "The Grants will do it." She takes her coat off the back of the chair, puts her arms in the sleeves, and starts to button up. "Why don't you have one of the muffins? I bought oranges yesterday, or you could have toast or frozen waffles."

~~Because I can't let myself want them~~ because I don't need a muffin (410), I don't want an orange (75) or toast (87), and waffles (180) make me gag.

I point to the empty bowl on the counter, next to the huddle of pill bottles and the Bluberridazzlepops box. "I'm having cereal."

Her eyes dart to the cabinet where she had taped up my meal plan. It came with the discharge papers when I moved in six months ago. I took it down three months later, on my eighteenth birthday.

"That's too small to be a full serving," she says carefully.

~~I could eat the entire box~~ I probably won't even fill the bowl. "My stomach's upset."

She opens her mouth again. Hesitates. A sour puff

of coffee-stained morning breath blows across the still kitchen and splashes into me. *Don't say it—don'tsayit.*

"Trust, Lia."

She said it.

"That's the issue. Especially now. We don't want . . ."

If I weren't so tired, I'd shove *trust* and *issue* down the garbage disposal and let it run all day.

I pull a bigger bowl out of the dishwasher and put it on the counter. "I. Am. Fine. Okay?"

She blinks twice and finishes buttoning her coat. "Okay. I understand. Tie your sneakers, Emma, and get in the car."

Emma yawns.

"Hang on." I bend down and tie Emma's laces. Double-knotted. I look up. "I can't keep doing this, you know. You're way too old."

She grins and kisses my forehead. "Yes you can, silly."

As I stand up, Jennifer takes two awkward steps toward me. I wait. She is a pale, round moth, dusted with eggshell foundation, armed for the day with her banker's briefcase, purse, and remote starter for the leased SUV. She flutters, nervous.

I wait.

This is where we should hug or kiss or pretend to.

She ties the belt around her middle. "Look . . . just keep moving today. Okay? Try not to think about things too much."

"Right."

"Say good-bye to your sister, Emma," Jennifer prompts.

"Bye, Lia." Emma waves and gives me a small berri-dazzle smile. "The cereal is really good. You can finish the box if you want."

◀ 003.00 ▶

I pour too much cereal (150) in the bowl, splash on the two-percent milk (125). Breakfast is themostimportant-mealoftheday. Breakfast will make me a cham-pee-on.

. . . When I was a real girl, with two parents and one house and no blades flashing, breakfast was granola topped with fresh strawberries, always eaten while reading a book propped up on the fruit bowl. At Cassie's house we'd eat waffles with thin syrup that came from maple trees, not the fake corn syrup stuff, *and we'd read the funny pages. . . .*

No. I can't go there. I won't think. I won't look.

I won't pollute my insides with Bluberridazzlepops or muffins or scritchscratchy shards of toast, either. Yesterday's dirt and mistakes have moved through me. I am shiny and pink inside, clean. Empty is good. Empty is strong.

But I have to drive.

. . . I drove last year, windows down, music cranked, first Saturday in October, flying to the SATs. I drove so Cassie could put the top coat on her nails. We were secret sisters with a plan for world domination, potential bubbling around us like champagne. Cassie laughed. I laughed. We were perfection.

Did I eat breakfast? Of course not. Did I eat dinner the night before, or lunch, or anything?

The car in front of us braked as the traffic light turned yellow, then red. My flip-flop hovered above the pedal. My edges blurred. Black squiggle tingles curled up my spine and wrapped around my eyes like a silk scarf. The car in front of us disappeared. The steering wheel, the dashboard, vanished. There was no Cassie, no traffic light. How was I supposed to stop this thing?

Cassie screamed in slow motion.

::Marshmallow/air/explosion/bag::

When I woke up, the emt-person and a cop were frowning. The driver whose car I smashed into was screaming into his cell phone.

My blood pressure was that of a cold snake. My heart was tired. My lungs wanted a nap. They stuck me with a needle, inflated me like a state-fair balloon, and shipped me off to a hospital with steel-eyed nurses who wrote down every bad number. In pen. Busted me.

Mom and Dad rushed in, side by side for a change, happy that I was not dead. A nurse handed my chart to my mother. She read through it and explained the disaster to my father and then they fought, a mudslide of an argument that spewed across the antiseptic sheets and out into the hall. I was stressed/overscheduled/manic/ no—depressed/no—in need of attention/no—in need of discipline/in need of rest/in need/your fault/your fault/ fault/fault. They branded their war on this tiny skin-bag of a girl.

Phone calls were made. My parents force-marched me into ~~hell on the hill~~ New Seasons. . . .

Cassie escaped, as usual. Not a scratch. Insurance more than covered the damage, so she wound up with a fixed car and new speakers. Our mothers had a little talk, but really all girls go through these things and what are you going to do? Cassie rescheduled for the next test and got her nails done at a salon, Enchanted Blue, *while they locked me up and dripped sugar water into my empty veins. . . .*

Lesson learned. Driving requires fuel.

Not Emma's Bluberridazzlepop cereal. I shiver and pour most of the soggy mess down the disposal, then set the bowl on the floor. Emma's cats, Kora and Pluto, pad across the kitchen and stick their heads in the bowl. I draw a cartoon face with a big tongue on a sticky note, write

YUMMY, EMMA! THANKS! and slap it on the cereal box.

I eat ten raisins (16) and five almonds (35) and a green-bellied pear (121) (= 172). The bites crawl down my throat. I eat my vitamins and the crazy seeds that keep my brain from exploding: one long purple, one fat white, two poppy-red. I wash everybody down with hot water.

They better work quick. The voice of a dead girl is waiting for me on my phone.

◀ 004.00 ▶

The climb upstairs takes longer than usual.

I sleep at the far end of the hall, in the tiny space still decorated like a guest room. White walls. Yellow curtains. The sofa bed is never folded up, the desk came from a yard sale. Jennifer keeps offering to buy me new furniture, and paint or put up wallpaper. I tell her I haven't figured out what I want to do yet. I should probably unpack the stacks of dusty boxes first.

My phone is waiting on top of the pile of dirty clothes, right where it landed when I chucked it at the wall early Sunday morning because the constant ringing was making me crazy and I was too tired to turn it off.

. . . *The last time she called* me was six months ago, after I got out of the hospital for the second time. I'd been calling her four or five times a day, but she wouldn't pick up or call me back, until finally, she did.

She asked me to listen and told me this wouldn't take long.

I was the root of all evil, Cassie said. A negative influence, a toxic shadow. While I was locked up, her parents had dragged her to a doctor who washed her brain and weighed her down with pills and empty words. She needed to move on with her life, redefine her boundaries, she said. I was the reason she cut classes and failed French, the cause of everything nasty and dangerous.

Wrong. Wrong. Wrong.

I was the reason she didn't run away freshman year. I was the reason she didn't eat a bottle of sleeping pills when her boyfriend cheated on her. I listened for hours when her parents yelled and tried to stuff her into a mannequin shell that didn't fit. I understood what triggered her earthquakes, most of them. I knew how much it hurt to be the daughter of people who can't see you, not even if you are standing in front of them stomping your feet.

But remembering all that was too complicated for Cassie. It was easier for her to dump me one last time. She turned my summer into a desert wasteland. When school started, she looked right through me in the halls, her new friends draped around her neck like Mardi Gras necklaces. *She wiped me off the face of her existence.*

❋ ❋ ❋

But something happened. In the dead time between Saturday night and Sunday morning, she called me.

Of course I didn't pick up. She was drunk-dialing, or prank-dialing. I wasn't going to let her sucker me into being her friend again just so she could turn around and crush me one more time.

. . . body found in a motel room, alone . . .

I didn't pick up. I didn't listen to her messages yesterday. I was too angry to even look at the phone.

She's still waiting for me.

I sit down on the mound of unwashed pajama bottoms and sweatshirts and dig out the phone. Open it. Cassie called thirty-three times, starting at 11:30 Saturday night.

RETRIEVE VOICE MAIL

"Lia? It's me. Call me."

Cassie.

Second message: "Where are you? Call me back." Cassie.

Third: "I'm not playing, Overbrook. I really need to talk to you."

Cassie, two days ago, Saturday.

"Call me."

"Please, please, call me."

"Look, I'm sorry I was such a bitch. Please."

"I know you're getting these messages."

"You can be mad at me later, okay? I really need to talk to you."

"You were right—it wasn't your fault."

"There's nobody else to talk to."

"Oh, God."

From 1:20 to 2:55, she hung up fifteen times.

Next: "Please, Lia-Lia." Her voice was slurring.

"I'm so sad. I can't get out."

"Call me. It's a mess."

Two more hang-ups.

3:20, very slurred: "I don't know what to do."

3:27. "I miss you. Miss you."

I bury the phone at the bottom of the pile and put on a heavier sweatshirt before I head for my car. Winter comes early in New Hampshire.

◀ 005.00 ▶

My timing is perfect, and I wind up in a traffic jam. The cars around me are driven by fat cows and bellowing bulls. We roll along, six mph. I can run faster than this. We brake. They chew their cud and moo into their phones until the herd shifts gears and rolls forward again.

Fifteen miles an hour. I can't run that fast.

Somewhere between Martins Corner and Route 28, I begin to cry. I turn on the radio, sing at the top of my lungs, turn it off again. I beat the steering wheel with my fists until I can see the bruises, and with every mile, I cry harder. Rain pours down my face.

> . . . body found in a motel room, alone . . .

What was she doing there? What was she thinking? Did it hurt?

There's no point in asking why, even though everybody will. I know why. The harder question is "why not?" I can't believe she ran out of answers before I did.

I need to run, to fly, beating my wings so hard I can't hear anything over the pounding of my heart. Rain, rain, rain, drowning me.

Was it easy?

I do not take any shortcuts, I do not forget to turn at the deli on the corner, I do not get lost, not even on purpose. I arrive at school on autopilot; late by their standards, early by mine. The last buses have just pulled up to the front door.

I get out and lock the car.

The unforgiving November wind blows me toward the building. Pointy snowflakes spiral down from the cake-frosting clouds overhead. The first snow. Magic. Everybody stops and looks up. The bus exhaust freezes, trapping all the noise in a gritty cloud. The doors to the school freeze, too.

We tilt back our heads and open wide.

The snow drifts into our zombie mouths crawling with grease and curses and tobacco flakes and cavities and boyfriend/girlfriend juice, the stain of lies. For one moment we are not failed tests and broken condoms and cheating on essays; we are crayons and lunch boxes and swinging so high our sneakers punch holes in the clouds. For one breath everything feels better.

Then it melts.

The bus drivers rev their engines and the ice cloud shatters. Everyone shuffles forward. They don't know what just happened. They can't remember.

she called me.

I walk back to my car, get in, turn on the heat, and wipe my face on my shirt. 7:30. Emma is done with French now and is unpacking her violin. She'll spend too much time rosining her bow, and not enough tuning the strings. The Winter Concert is coming up in a few weeks, and she doesn't know the songs yet. I should help her with that.

Cassie's at the morgue, I guess. Last night she slept there in a silver drawer, eyes getting used to the dark.

Jennifer said they're doing an autopsy. Who will cut off her clothes? Will they give her a bath, strangers touching her skin? Can she watch them? Will she cry?

The late bell rings, and the last people in the parking lot sprint for the door. Just a few minutes more. I can't go in until the halls are empty and the teachers have numbed them with boredom so they won't notice when I slip down the halls.

I turn around and clear a place in the backseat, shoving all the tests, sweatshirts, and overdue library books to one side so Emma will have a place to sit when I pick her up. Jennifer insists on sticking her in the back. It's safer, she says.

There is no safer. There's not even safe, never has been.

Cassie thought heaven was a fairy tale for stupid people. How can you find a place you don't believe in? You can't. So where does she go now? What if she comes back, eyes on angryfire?

7:35. Time to go to school and stop thinking.

◀ **006.00** ▶

No Honors Option for me, not this year. I am Contemp World Lit, Soc Sci 12—The Holocaust, Physics, Trig (again), and Lunch. No gym, thanks to a magic note from Dr. Parker. There are asterisks next to my name and footnotes that explain the situation.

. . . *When I was a real girl*, my mother fed me her glass dreams one spoonful at a time. Harvard. Yale.

Princeton. Duke. Undergrad. Med school. Internship, residency, God. She'd brush my hair and braid it with long words, weaving the Latin roots and Greek branches into my head so memorizing anatomy would come easy. ~~Mom~~ Dr. Marrigan was furious when the guidance counselor kicked me out of Honors and dropped me down to College Track. The counselor suggested that I plan on going to my father's college, because they had to let me in. Free tuition for faculty kids, she reminded us.

I was relieved.

That night Dr. Marrigan told me that I was too smart to be a slacker faculty kid. She wanted to have me privately tested, to prove that I was brilliant and that the school was not meeting my needs. But then I screwed up again and they slammed me back in the hospital and when I got out, I changed all the rules.

I used to fantasize about taking the Mensa test to prove that I wasn't a total loser. Maybe I'd score total off-the-hook genius. I'd make one hundred thousand photocopies of the test results, glue them to the walls of my mother's house, take a bucket of red paint and a thick brush, and I'd write HA! a million times.

But there was a pretty good chance I'd flunk it. *I really didn't want to know.*

The buzzer sounds. Students float from room to room. The teachers tie us to our chairs and pour worlds into our ears.

The shades are pulled and the lights are off in the physics lab so we can watch a movie about the speed of light and the speed of sound and some other garbage that doesn't matter. Ghosts are waiting in the shadows of the room, patient dull shimmers. The others can see them, too, I know it. We're all afraid to talk about what stares at us from the dark.

Waves of physics particles stream through the room.

she called me thirty-three times.

A ghost wraps herself around me, strokes my hair, and puts me to sleep.

The buzzer sounds. My classmates grab their books and race for the door. I have drooled on the desk.

My physics teacher (what is his name?) frowns at me. When he breathes through his open mouth, I can smell the night scum coating his tongue and the sunny-side-up eggs he ate for breakfast. "Are you planning on staying here all day?" he asks.

I shake my head no. Before he tries to be witty again, I grab my books and stand up. *Too fast.* The floor tries to pull me down face-first, but my night-scummy teacher is watching so I make myself strong enough to float away, stars swimming in my eyes.

1.2.3.4.5.6.7.8.9.10.11.12.13.14.15.16.17.18.19.

20.21.22.23.24.25.26.27.28.29.30.31.32.33.

❋ ❋ ❋

"Dead girl walking," the boys say in the halls.

"Tell us your secret," the girls whisper, one toilet to another.

I am *that* girl.

I am the space between my thighs, daylight shining through.

I am the library aide who hides in Fantasy.

I am the circus freak encased in beeswax.

I am the bones they want, wired on a porcelain frame.

When I get close, they step back. The cameras in their eyeholes record the zit on my chin, the rain in my eyes, the blue water under my skin. They pick up every sound on their collar microphones. They want to pull me inside of them, but they're afraid.

I am contagious.

I tiptoe to the nurse's office, hand on the wall to keep me vertical. If I run or breathe too deep, the cheap stitches holding me together will snap, and all the stickiness inside will pour out and burn through the concrete.

The nurse ruffles her feathers when I slink in. She turns down the radio, cool jazz, and looks me over, hands on her hips, eyes sad and friendly.

"I thought you might stay home today," she says. "It's got to be a shock. Cassie was real close to you, wasn't she?"

"I don't feel good," I say. "Can I lie down for a while?"

"You know the rules."

She is a crafty witch in nurse's clothing.

"Okay." I sit on the chair next to her desk and let her take my temperature and blood pressure.

She wraps the cuff around my arm bone. "Are you still being weighed regularly?"

"Once a week. I'm fine. I don't need to step on your scale."

"You don't look fine." She jots down my numbers. "If you're going to stay here, you have to get something in your system. If you don't, it's back to class."

Do I want to die from the inside out or the outside in?

She opens up a carton of orange juice, pours it into a paper cup, and hands it to me as she removes the thermometer. "I'm serious."

I take the cup from her. ~~My throat wants it my brain wants it my blood wants it~~ my hand does not want this my mouth does not want this.

The nurse wants this and I need to hide. I force it down.

The door opens and two guys walk in; one bleeding from his nose, the other looking a little freaked out at the sight of blood. The nurse makes the bleeder sit with his head tilted back and his buddy sit with his head between his knees so he doesn't pass out.

I throw the paper cup in the trash can, take the newspaper off her desk, and retreat to the cot at the far end of the room.

"You'll drink another one in fifteen minutes," the nurse says. "Or you can have a lollipop: grape or lime."

"Right."

I pull the little screen in front of the cot, sit down, and search through the newspaper. Local section, page 2. The article runs for a couple of inches, next to an ad for fur coats, thirty percent off.

Police are investigating the death of 19-year-old Cassandra Parrish, of the town of Amoskeag, NH, whose body was discovered early Sunday morning in a room of the Gateway Motel on River Road in Centerville. Authorities were called to the scene at 4:43 A.M. by the motel employee who found the body. Preliminary indications suggest Miss Parrish may have died of natural causes, but police have not yet ruled out foul play or drug use.

"We're still gathering information," said police spokesperson Sgt. Anna Warren. "We'll have a report about the time and cause of death when the coroner finishes the autopsy."

Miss Parrish, known to friends as Cassie, was a popular athlete and member of the theater club at Amoskeag High. Her father, Jerry Parrish, is the principal of Park Street Elementary School, and her mother, Cindy, is active in school and community affairs. Amoskeag Superintendent of Schools Nelson Bushnel said the Parrish family's loss was "heartbreaking."

"Cassie was what we all want our children to be:

bright, hardworking, and kind," said Bushnell. When asked to comment on reports that Miss Parrish had a troubled background, he said, "Most teens today struggle with something. Cassie had made great strides in embracing a healthy life. The last time I talked to her father, he said she was trying to choose between studying psychology or French literature in college. Her death is as tragic as it is shocking."

Autopsy results are expected later in the week. Funeral plans were incomplete at press time.

I lie down on the cot, the paper pillowcase crackling in my ears like radio static.

The buzzer sounds. The hall fills with a river of bodies and voices whispering that Cassie was murdered/no, she hung herself/no, she smoked or snorted her way to the Final Exit. She'd try anything once, did you hear about the time under the bleachers/at the mall/at summer camp? She drove herself into a speeding train/jumped without a parachute/strapped on a weight belt and dove into the ocean.

She offered herself to the big, bad wolf and didn't scream when he took the first bite.

. . . body found in a motel room, alone . . .

The boys are gone. The nurse takes the newspaper away and spreads a thin blanket over me.

"Can I get another one?" I ask. "I'm cold."

"Sure thing." She walks to the supply closet, her shoes squeaking on the polished floor.

"Have you heard anything about the funeral?" I ask.

"The superintendent's office sent an e-mail," she says. "The viewing will be Wednesday night at St. Stephen's. They'll bury her on Saturday." She walks toward me, her arms loaded down. "Get some sleep now and remember: you're drinking more orange juice when you wake up."

"I promise."

She covers me with all of the blankets she has (five) and the jackets from the lost-and-found box, because I am freezing. I drift into the armpits of strangers, tasting their manic salt, and sleep to forget everything.

◀ 007.00 ▶

Emma is buckled in the backseat watching a movie on the DVD player in her lap, eating potato chips and pounding a Mountain Dew slushie.

"Don't tell Jennifer," I say.

"Uh-huh."

"Seriously. She'll yell."

"I heard you. Don't tell or she'll yell." Emma's eyes are glued to the screen, the chips moving one at a time into her mouth on a pink conveyor belt.

We're lost. Again. My father doesn't want me to get a GPS because he says I have to learn how to get around on my own. How can I figure out where I'm going if I'm lost all the time? I'll ask Jennifer. Christmas is coming.

We pass a dying barn with a shattered roof, and a stained mattress shoved up against the speed-limit sign. Wouldn't you notice if a mattress fell off your car? Maybe it was in the back of a truck loaded down with everything a girl owned, taking her to some guy she met online. She promised him her body and soul. He promised her three meals a day and a house but said the place could use more furniture. He didn't stop when the mattress fell off. A new wife deserves a clean bed, that's what he always said.

Maybe a leather-covered biker girl, butch and strong, is coming down the road a mile or so behind me. Any minute now, some idiot will cut in front of her and she'll swerve and the bike will flip and send her screaming because she forgot her wings again and gravity never forgets

and then she'll hit

that nasty mattress. And yeah, she'll wind up with three broken ribs, a fractured femur, and a strained neck, but the ambulance drivers won't ever mention that. They'll always talk about how the stained mattress at the side of the road saved that chick's life.

The smell of Emma's potato chips is doing this to my brain.

❋ ❋ ❋

By the time I find the Richland Park fields, practice has already started. Emma wants to stay in the car until the end of the movie.

"You need to get out there," I say.

She groans and closes the player. "I hate soccer."

"So tell them you want to quit."

"Mom says the season is almost over and I'm not allowed."

"So get out there and play. Have fun."

She looks at my eyes in the rearview mirror. "Nobody ever kicks me the ball."

Emma is a mattress who got thrown off the truck when her parents split up. I can't remember the last time her father called. Jennifer is determined to carve her into the perfect-little-girl who will turn into the perfect-young-lady whose shining accomplishments will prove to the world that Jennifer is the absolutely perfect mother.

It's not like you can blame a mattress when people don't tie it down tight enough.

I open my door. "Come on. I'll kick the ball to you."

She closes the player and tosses it on the seat. "No, you said you have homework." She suddenly can't get out fast enough. "Bye, Lia. Drive safe."

It takes a couple of heartbeats to figure out what just happened. *One. Two. Three.* The smells are messing with my neurons again.

I roll down the window. "Emma. Hang on."

She slowly walks back to the car, hugging the soccer ball tight. "What?"

"I changed my mind. I want to watch you practice. Where should I sit?"

Her eyes fly open. "No, you can't."

"Why not? Other people are watching."

"Um, it's just . . ." She looks at her cleats and mumbles. "You can watch from the car. It's warmer."

There are shouts from the field, nine-year-olds psyching themselves up for the kill. Travel soccer is intense.

"Emma, look at me." How did Jennifer's voice sneak into my throat? "Why don't you want me to get out of the car?"

She kicks the gravel. Tiny stones bounce up and ding the paint on my door.

"Coach asked me if it was true you had cancer." She kicks again. "'Cause he heard you were in the hospital and . . . you know. I said yes." Whistles blow on the field. "I'm sorry. I didn't know what else to say."

"It's okay," I say. "I understand. Don't worry about it."

The ball slips out of her hands and rolls toward the field. "You're not mad at me?"

"I can never be mad at you, silly."

She finally looks up. "Thanks, Lia."

"And you're right, I have a ton of homework." I start the engine. "My teachers will love you for making me deal with it. See you later?"

She smiles. "Okay. I think there are some chips left, if you're hungry."

I roll up the window.

I wish I had cancer.

I will burn in hell for that, but it's true.

◀ 008.00 ▶

The air at the gas station is heavy with diesel and the smell of rancid deep-fryer fat from the McDonald's next door. Five days ago I weighed 101.30 pounds. I had to eat at Thanksgiving (vultures all around the table), but since then it's been mostly water and rice cakes. ~~I am so hungry that I could gnaw off my right hand.~~ I stick three pieces of gum in my mouth, throw out Emma's potato chips, and fill the tank. I am disgusting.

. . . *The first time they admitted me,* I was black and blue and purple and red because I passed out and hit the car in front of us while Cassie screamed and the steering wheel exploded. This body weighed 093.00 pounds.

My roommate at ~~the prison~~ New Seasons was a long, withered zucchini who cried in bed and let the snot run down the sides of her face. Everybody on the staff was whale-sized and sweaty. The nurse who handed out meds was so fat her skin was stretched tight. If she moved too fast, it would rip open and her yellow stuffing would spill out, ruining her Disney World sweatshirt.

I bit the days off in rows, corn kernels that popped in my mouth and wedged between my teeth. Bite. Chew. Swallow. Again. Bite. Chew. Swallow. Again.

I was a good girl because I didn't poke holes in my skin (scars noted) or write depressing poetry (journals checked while we were in session) and I ate and ate. They stuffed me like a pink little piggy ready for market. They killed me with mushy apples and pasta worms and little cakes that marched out of the oven and lay down to be frosted. I bit, chewed, swallowed day after day and lied, lied, lied. (Who wants to recover? It took me years to get that tiny. I wasn't sick; I was strong.) But staying strong would keep me locked up. The only way out was to shove in food until I waddled.

I hawked up crap from the back of my throat about feelings and issues and my thighs. The docs nodded and gave me stickers for my honesty. Four weeks later, the gates opened. ~~Mom~~ Dr. Marrigan drove me ~~home~~ to her house and we pretended none of it ever happened, except for the meal plans and the rules and the appointments and the scales and the hurricane of my mother's disappointment.

Cassie understood. She listened to everything that happened *and she told me I was brave. . . .*

I pull into the garage, brain dripping with gasoline fumes. I don't remember driving home. One of these days

I'm going to walk into the house and the news guy on TV will be reporting a hit-and-run that just happened downtown. The camera will show blood and broken glass on the sidewalk. A reporter will interview a sobbing woman who saw the accident in front of the department store on Bartlett Street. I'll have a funny taste in my mouth because I'll be holding a shopping bag from that store in my hand. I will run back to the garage and find the dead body of a woman stuck in my windshield, blood everywhere.

This kind of thing can happen.

I get out and check the whole car—check the doors, hood, bumpers, lights, front grill, and trunk to make sure I didn't get into an accident without noticing. No broken lights or dented doors. No dead ladies in the windshield. Not today.

◀ 009.00 ▶

I head straight for the refrigerator and pull out the leftover Thanksgiving stuffing.

. . . *When I was a real girl*, Thanksgiving was at Nanna Marrigan's house in Maine, or Grandma Overbrook's in Boston. At Nanna's we ate oyster stuffing. At Grandma's it was chestnut and sausage. Nanna liked her pumpkin pie on a cinnamon-pecan crust. Grandma's pies had to be mincemeat because that's what her grandmother did. The tables were crowded with tall people reaching for bowls of food and talking too loud; cousins and great-uncles and friends from far away. The smell of gravy and onions made my parents forget to fight, the taste of cranberries reminded them how to laugh. My grandmothers were going to live forever, and Thanksgiving would always be lace tablecloths, thin china, and heavy silver that I stood on a stool to polish.

They died.

Last week's Thanksgiving was artificially sweetened, enriched with tense preservatives, and wrapped in plastic. Dad's sisters don't come anymore because it's too far. Jennifer's family goes to her brother's because he has more bedrooms. (~~Mom~~ Dr. Marrigan probably ate at her desk, or took a symbolic scoop of mashed potatoes and gravy in the hospital cafeteria.)

We were us four, plus two of my father's grad students. One was a vegan; she ate three helpings of yams and most of the pumpkin bread that she brought. The guy was from Los Angeles. He said he was fasting because Thanksgiving honors the genocide of America's native peoples. After they left, Emma asked Dad why the fasting guy came at all. Dad said he was sucking up to get a letter of recommendation. Jennifer said *she hoped he choked on it.*

I dump some of Jennifer's stuffing on a plate, drop a couple spoonfuls on the floor for the cats, then squish ketchup on top and heat it in the microwave long enough for the ketchup to splatter all over. I leave the microwave door hanging open so the smell pollutes the kitchen.

Check the clock. Ten minutes.

I dab a little ketchup at the corners of my mouth, scrape the entire mess into the garbage disposal, turn on the hot water, and flick the switch. While the disposal is running, I try to detour my mind—*recite the Constitution, list the presidents in order, remember the names of the seven dwarfs*—I can't stop thinking that

she called me.

I close the microwave. Carry the dirty plate and fork to the family room, where I put them on an end table.

Seven minutes.

I really do have to eat.

she called me thirty-three times.

One large rice cake = 35. Top it with one teaspoon of spicy mustard and you add 5. Two teaspoons = 10. Rice cakes with hot sauce are better. You eat and are punished in the same bite. Jennifer doesn't buy hot sauce anymore. Two rice cakes, four teaspoons of mustard = 90.

I wish I was a puker. I try and try and try, but I can't do it. The smell freaks me out and my throat closes and I just can't.

1.2.3.4.5.6.7.8.9.10.11.12.13.14.15.16.17.18.19.

20.21.22.23.24.25.26.27.28.29.30.31.32.33.

Jennifer comes home and asks me to put my plate in the dishwasher and clean up the mess I made in the microwave. I apologize and do what she asks while she struggles to open a slippery bottle of cold Chardonnay. When I'm halfway up the stairs, Emma bursts through the front door, soccer uniform dirty, cheeks red.

"I almost scored a goal!" she shouts.

"Awesome," I say.

"You want to kick the ball with me now?"

Too many ropes pulling me down into the ground. "I can't, Emmakins. I'm buried. Besides, it's already dark. Tomorrow, okay?"

The edges of her smile crumble. I pull myself up the rest of the stairs.

Close the door. Close the door.

My knitting basket is one of the few things I bothered to unpack when I moved here. I sit on the edge of my bed and dig into it, past the never-ending scarf/blanket project, past mateless needles and woolly balls of orange and brown and red, to the magic bottle of blush-colored Emergency Only pills. Cassie got them for me, but she wouldn't say where they came from. I take one, only one.

Plastic stars wait on the cold ceiling, watching the light switch, nervous, ready for the dark and their cue to glow. This girl has Physics homework. This girl has a paper on genocide to write and last week's Trig problems, and a makeup quiz about literary devices in some stupid story.

This girl shivers and crawls under the covers with all her clothes on and falls into an overdue library book, a faerie story with rats and marrow and burning curses. The sentences build a fence around her, a Times Roman 10-point barricade, to keep the thorny voices in her head from getting too close.

When Dad comes home, the microwave heats his supper. More wine is poured. Jennifer tells Emma that it's past her bedtime. I turn page after quiet page, but I've stopped seeing the letters, stopped understanding the words.

His footsteps on the stairs.

I arrange my face in the middle of the book, my hair spread like seaweed floating in the current of the story that sweeps me under and away to sleep. I drape a loose hand over the edge of the bed.

No, better not. I pull the hand back in.

His footsteps in the hall. Door opens.

"Lia?"

Lia is not available. Please leave a message when you hear the beep.

she called me thirty-three times.

✳ ✳ ✳

"Lia? Are you awake?"

Jennifer uses the cranky-Mommy voice to tell Emma "for the last time get up those stairs." Emma's answer is too quiet to be heard.

Dad sits on the edge of my bed. He brushes the hair off my face, leans forward, and kisses my forehead. He smells like leftovers and wine.

"Lia?"

Go away. Lia needs to sleep for one hundred years in a locked glass box. The people who know where the key is hidden will die and she'll finally get some rest.

He lifts my head and slides the book out from under it. I open one eye a slit and watch through the spiky lashes. He marks my place by bending a corner of the page, then reads the stuff on the back. Above his collar, the skin jumps, the blood rushing to feed his giant brain.

My father is a history professor, the Great and Powerful Expert about the American Revolution. He's won a Pulitzer, a National Book Award, and a job consulting on a cable news show. The White House invites him for dinner so often that he owns a tuxedo. He has played squash with two vice presidents and a secretary of defense. He knows how we became who we are today and where we should go from here. My teachers tell me I should feel lucky to have a father like this. Maybe if I didn't hate history, I would.

"Lia? I know you're awake. We need to talk."

I stop breathing.

"I'm sorry about Cassie, honey."

The glass around me crackles. Cassie called me before she died. She called and called and called and waited for me to pick up.

1.2.3.4.5.6.7.8.9.10.11.12.13.14.15.16.17.18.19.
20.21.22.23.24.25.26.27.28.29.30.31.32.33.

My father smoothes my hair again. "Thank God you're safe."

Fracture lines etch the surface of the glass box as if a body fell from the sky and landed on it. He doesn't hear the impact, can't smell the blood.

He takes a deep breath and pats my shoulder hidden under the comforter. "We'll talk later," he lies.

We never talk. We just pretend to think about talking, and we mention from time to time that one of these days, we really should sit down and talk. It'll never happen.

The bed creaks as he stands. He turns off the light on the nightstand and crosses the room in the dim glow of the plastic galaxy glued overhead. The *snick* of the tongue of the catch finding its place in the door frame releases me.

I roll to face the wall. Shards of glass race for my heart because Cassie is dead and cold. She died in the Gateway Motel and it is my fault. Not the magazines or the Web sites, or the knife-tongue girls in the locker room, or the neck-sucking boys on the back porch. Not her coaches or directors or counselors or the inventors of size 0 and 00. Not even her mother or her father.

i didn't answer.

◀ 010.00 ▶

. . .*When I was a real girl, my best friend was named Cassandra Jane Parrish.* She moved in the winter of third grade. I sat with my chin on the windowsill and stared across the street as they unloaded the moving van. A guy carried out a kid-sized bike and a pink plastic dollhouse. I crossed my fingers. Our development was still raw, mostly unfinished skeleton houses and freezing pits of mud. I was dying for somebody my age to play with.

My babysitter walked me and a pot of coffee across to meet the new people. The house was exactly like ours only flipped backwards, with the same smell of new paint and clean carpets. The mom, Mrs. Parrish, looked old enough to be a grandmother. She had blue eyes that stayed wide open all the time, like she was surprised by everything she saw. The babysitter introduced me and explained about my parents and their million-hour-a-week jobs. Mrs. Parrish called upstairs to her daughter. Cassandra Jane shouted back that she was never coming out of her room.

"Go on up, dear," Mrs. Parrish said to me. "I know she wants a friend."

Cassie was unpacking a box of paperbacks. When she stood up, she was a head taller than me with long blonde hair that curlicued down her back. At first she wouldn't talk, wouldn't even look me in the eye, but she let me hold her mouse, Pinky. His beating heart vibrated against my fingertips.

Her room was the same size and shape as mine, but filled with different stuff: a canopy bed fringed with lace curtains, the dollhouse marked with black crayon scribbles, a tall, skinny mirror that stood by itself in the corner, and a bookcase that didn't look big enough to hold all those boxes of books. She showed me her antique dolls and plastic horse collection, and best of all, a real treasure chest that had rubies and gold and a piece of green sea-glass born in the heart of a volcano.

I told her that sea-glass came from the ocean.

"This is different," she said. "It's 'see-glass,' like seeing with your eyes. If you look through it when the stars line up right, you can see your future."

"Oh," I said, reaching for it.

"But not today." She put the see-glass away and locked the treasure chest. I saw where she hid the key.

We sat down with a box between us and started unpacking. As I handed her book after book, we compared favorite series and authors and then movies and TV shows and music that we pretended to listen to, even though it was way too old for us. When Mrs. Parrish and my babysitter came in, Cassie put her arm around my shoulder.

"It's fate," she told her mom. "We were meant to be friends."

Mrs. Parrish smiled. "I told you things would be fine here."

Cassie's dad was our new principal, hired from upstate after the old one had a stroke. Her mom became our Girl Scout troop leader and the volunteer who chaperoned field trips and sewed costumes for the school play. She invited my mother over for cards and scrapbooking parties and book club meetings, but Mom was too busy transplanting hearts. Mr. Parrish didn't play squash; my dad didn't golf, so that was that.

Cassie was a little moody, but I got used to it. I slept over at her house almost every weekend, but she never slept at mine. She wouldn't talk about her sleepwalking or the temper tantrums that exploded when her mother nagged her or her father made her do her chores over again.

Once I heard her mother talking to my babysitter about something bad that had happened in their old neighborhood, something with a boy. I asked Cassie about it. She said I was trying to hurt her feelings and she hated me and we weren't friends anymore. I sat on my front steps, reading *A Wrinkle in Time* and gnawing on the end of my ponytail, until she came back an hour later, like nothing had happened, and asked me to ride bikes with her.

Every afternoon in the summer we'd crawl into my tree house to read armloads of books filled with great quests and dangerous adventures. I made swords out of branches, sharpening the tips with a steak knife stolen from the kitchen. Cassie picked poisonous berries and cut a rose from her mother's garden. We smeared the berries on our faces and pricked our fingers on a thorn. We swore sacred oaths to be strong and to save the planet and to be friends forever.

She taught me how to play solitaire. I taught her how to play hearts.

In the spring of fifth grade, the boob fairy arrived with her wand and smacked Cassie wicked hard. She became the first girl in our class to really need a bra. The boys stared and snickered. The glittering girls, the ones with split tongues and pinchy fingers, whispered. I was secretly glad for my skinny chest and undershirts.

The boys tried out their dirty words and crude comments on her for weeks. Cassie pretended she didn't hear them, but I knew. Things boiled over in the lunch line on a Friday. Thatcher Greyson snapped the back of Cassie's bra so hard everybody heard it. She whirled around, pushed him to the ground, jumped on him, and started pounding. By the time the aides pulled her off, he had a black eye and a bloody nose.

Thatcher went to the nurse. Cassie was sent to Mr. Parrish's office because he was the principal and her dad at the same time. He yelled at her so loud you could hear it in the hall, and then he sent her and Thatcher home for the day. The rest of us spent the afternoon writing essays about tolerance and kindness. This pissed off the glittering girls, who said it was all her fault.

On Monday, the girls declared that Cassie was a dyke lesbo and threw her out of the tribe. I didn't know what a dyke lesbo was, but it did not sound good. I chewed on the eraser end of my pencil and didn't talk to Cassie all day. She sat alone at lunch on Tuesday. Played alone at recess. Instead of taking the bus, she drove home with her mom.

On Wednesday the boys whispered a chant of "boobies, jugs, hooters, tits" whenever the teacher wasn't paying attention. Thatcher drew a picture of Cassie with watermelon-sized breasts and passed it around the class. The glittering girls giggled and twirled their gum around their fingers.

In the pecking order of fifth grade, I was closer to the top than the bottom because my parents were rich and my dad had met the president of the United States. In the complex math of elementary school, I was a whole number, not a fraction.

Cassie and me had taken a sacred oath with poison berry juice and blood. There was no choice to make. I had to save her.

At lunchtime, I sat next to Cassie at the loser end of the table. I gave her all my french fries and talked loudly about the two of us going to Boston for a museum trip with her mom. The other girls watched, tongues flicking over their braces, tasting their lip gloss and testing the wind.

At recess, I walked up to Thatcher; me—a scrawny elf girl the size of a small second-grader standing up to a future varsity football player, offensive tackle.

"I dare you to punch me," I said.

"You? Dare me?" He was laughing too hard to say anything else.

I shoved him. "I double-dare you. If you don't have the guts to do it, you're a weenie." I shoved again, harder. "If you do, you're an even bigger weenie because it's harder to take a punch than to give one."

I had no idea how those words snuck into my mouth.

Everybody said, "Ooooooooohhhhhh," and made a circle around us. Thatcher looked around for a teacher to save him. I closed my eyes and crossed my fingers.

"Do it," I said.

He punched me so hard my lip split open and the loose molar I had been teasing with my tongue broke off. I spit the bloody tooth into his face just before I passed out.

The glittering girls changed sides again. I had showed Thatcher. I had proved that girls rule. They made braided bracelets for me with embroidery thread and beads, but I wouldn't take them unless they made some for Cassie, too. They invited Cassie back in the tribe, because really, Thatcher was a bully and the whole thing was his fault.

After that, Cassie and me *always told people we were twins.*

. . . body found in a motel room, alone . . .

The body of Cassandra Jane Parrish is asleep in a cold silver box. They'll dig a hole in the ground and plant her on Saturday.

What about the rest of her, the real Cassie?

I think she's coming here.

◀ 011.00 ▶

Emma goes to bed and Jennifer goes to bed and Dad goes to bed. On the other side of town, my mother stays up too late, but she finally goes to bed, too.

I cannot sleep. Heat lightning shoots through my skull, short-circuiting the wires. I am cold, then hot, and then I can't feel my fingers or my toes. Someone is standing on the other side of my door. I can feel it. But . . . no. Everyone is sleeping. Everyone is enchanted, pulled under into a dream.

The moon drips through my window.

I wait.

Spiders hatch and crawl out of my belly button, hairy little tar beads with ballerina feet. They swarm, spinning a silk veil, one hundred thousand spider thoughts woven together until they wrap me up in a cozy shroud.

I breathe in. The web presses against my open lips. It tastes dusty, like old curtains.

The smell of ginger and cloves and burnt sugar drifts over my bed, the smell of her body wash and shampoo and perfume. She's coming. Any minute now.

I breathe out and it begins.

Thorn-covered vines creep across the floor, crackling like a bonfire. Black roses bloom in the moonlight, born dead and brittle. The web on my face holds my eyes open, forcing me to watch as Cassie steps out of the shadows, briars twining up her legs and around her body, reaching up through her hair. One minute she's by the door, the next, she stands over me. The temperature in the room has dropped twenty degrees. Her voice is in my head.

"Lia," she says.

I can't make a sound. Spiders crawl on my face and leap across to her arms. They fly back and forth, knitting us together.

"Come with me," she says. "Please."

The web locks us into place, staring at each other as the moon slithers across the sky and the stars fall asleep.

◀ 012.00 ▶

"Wake up, Lia!" Emma shakes my shoulder.

I groan and bury myself deeper in the warm cocoon.

"Wake up!" She turns on the light. "You're going to be late."

I open my eyes and raise my hand to block out the glare. I'm still wearing my clothes. It's dark outside. "What time is it?"

"Duh," says Emma. "After six thirty."

My room smells like dirty laundry and old candles, not spices or burnt sugar. I plant my face in the pillow. "Five more minutes."

"You have to get up now." She drags the comforter off me. "Mommy said."

"Hey! It's cold."

"Don't yell; Mommy has a migraine. I tried to wake you up nice, but you didn't move."

I swing my legs over the side of the bed and sit up. There are no spiderwebs in sight, no rose petals on the carpet. Cassie is in the morgue, belly slit and draining like a fresh-caught fish. It didn't happen.

I shiver, pull the comforter back up, and wrap it around my shoulders. "Where's my dad?"

"It's Tuesday, silly. Squash day. Why is squash the only vegetable that has a game named after it?"

Crap. Tuesday.

"Where's Jennifer?"

"Drying her hair. Where are you going?"

It's Tuesday.

I race downstairs to the laundry room, as far away from Jennifer's ears as I can get. I turn on the tap, lean over the sink, and guzzle until my belly is a big water balloon. I sail on the tide toward the kitchen, heavy-loaded with ballast, waves splashing.

When Jennifer comes down with dry hair and sloppy eyeliner, I'm on the first cup of coffee of the day. Black. I have Daddy's dirty plate in front of me so it looks like I ate toast and jam.

"Migraine?" I ask.

She nods once, winces, and puts a mug of water into the microwave.

My little not-sister shoves a shoe-box diorama across the table at me. "It's a coliseum in Greece," she says. "Where they tortured the people and fed them to the tigers."

"Sounds like middle school," I say.

"That is not funny," Jennifer says. "And it's the Roman Colosseum, in Rome, not Greece. Stop touching it, Emma. The glue isn't dry yet." The microwave beeps. She takes out the mug, plops in a tea bag that smells like lemons, glances at the clock, and says, "Come, on, Lia. Upstairs."

※ ※ ※

The second time they let me out of ~~prison New Seasons~~ *the clinic, six months ago,* I divorced ~~my mother~~ Dr. Marrigan and moved to jenniferland.

Once the shock wore off, Dad liked the idea. It would be a new start, he said. With a predictable routine and someone who knew how to cook. Every summer morning I did the good-daughter shuffle into the kitchen and sat at the breakfast table with my father (from the discharge papers: "family mealtimes should be light and pleasant"). He would lecture me about his latest research into the boring life of some dead guy while I ate tiny forkfuls of mushroom omelet and nibbles of cinnamon bagel with butter.

The doctors told Dad to buy a Blubber-O-Meter 3000, a bathroom scale with a giant dial that was easy to read. Jennifer had to do the dirty work, weighing me in my tattered yellow robe to make sure I stayed fat. For the first couple of months, she measured my sins every morning and called in the results to my doctor once a week. The ugly numbers made me cry.

Everyday weighing became every-other-day weighing *became every-Tuesday weighing because none of us wanted to do it in the first place.*

I change into the yellow robe in my bedroom and make sure the quarters I sewed into the pockets aren't making them droop. When I get to the bathroom, Jennifer is fixing her eyeliner in the mirror. I step on the scales.

107.00 fake pounds.

She writes the number in the little green notebook that lives in the cabinet next to the antibacterial ointment, then flips through twenty-four weeks of humiliating recorded weights. "That's down a quarter pound."

"Way above trouble, though."

"Um-hmm." The notebook goes back in the cabinet. The cover is beginning to tear off the spiral rings.

I step off the scale and change the subject. "Can I take Emma out for ice cream after school?"

The stepmouth opens, but no words come out.

Emma is nine. Emma is plump. Plump, not husky, not heavy, not fat. She is big-boned—like her dad, she says—and her plump is perfect. Emma should be a model; we've heard it a million times at school concerts and soccer tournaments. She is the new American average, a living-flesh girl with chocolate M&M eyes, and hair that bounces, and a roll of love around her tummy.

Jennifer thinks that Emma is ~~fat~~ plump, but she doesn't have the guts to say it.

"One scoop," I promise. "In a dish."

"Not today." Her lipstick is bleeding into the corners of her mouth. She pulls a tissue out of the box and leans into the mirror to repair the damage. It's an antique mirror with little waves on the surface of it. Sometimes it can make you look like an elegant princess trapped in time. Other times, it makes you look like a pig.

I pull back the shower curtain and turn on the water. Jennifer blot, blot, blots. "Chloe called," she says. "Again."

"Here?"

"No. David's office."

I make the water hotter. I do not like the shape of my mother's name in her mouth.

"Did you hear what I said?"

"You said Mom called Dad."

"You promised me yesterday that you'd call her."

I sit on the edge of the tub and test the temperature with my fingers. "I'm sorry. I forgot."

"Don't worry about it. She wants you to visit her this weekend, to spend the night. She said it's time for you two to try again, especially with Cassie's death. She's very worried about you."

"No."

Jennifer's reflection frowns at me. She's still learning how to pick her way through the bombed-out countryside that lies between her stepmess and the mythological Wife Number One. But she earns a star for trying.

She takes a deep breath. "I think it's a good idea."

"I don't."

"Come on, Lia, you should—"

"You're not supposed to say that." Steam billows. I want to strip and boil myself, but if she sees me naked, she'll freak, and if I get in the shower wearing my robe, she'll freak harder. "Dr. Parker says I don't have to let anyone 'should' on me."

"I'm sorry." She wipes a clear spot in the mirror. "I'm just trying to help."

"I know."

When she married my father, I was the once-a-month visitor who cleaned the kitchen without being told and babysat for free. I bet she wishes she had written an escape clause into the prenup.

"What did Dad tell Mom?" I ask.

"He said he'd talk to you."

The water falls, five gallons a minute down the drain. Jennifer is fading behind the wall of steam.

"Just go for one night." Her voice is sticky, like the lipstick bled on her tongue. "Get there at dinnertime on Saturday, come home after breakfast."

I open my mouth to ask her to go with me to the funeral, to go to the wake tomorrow, to help me figure out if I should call Cassie's parents or if that would make things worse. I open my mouth, but steam rushes in and boils away the words.

"Did you say something?" she asks.

"Are you going to the store today?"

"What?"

"Are you going to the store? I'm out of tampons." Total lie, brilliant diversion.

"Sure. I'll pick some up. You'll call Chloe?"

"I'll call her this afternoon. Now, if you don't mind ..."
I stand up and reach for the belt of my robe.

She steps into the hall, half closing the door. "Thanks,
honey. I'll tell David."

I stare into the steam until I know she's down the
stairs.

"Don't call me 'honey.'"

◀ 013.00 ▶

I turn off the shower. Clouds hang in the air. Tears roll
down the mirror, the walls, and the windows. I wait for
the magical sound of the garage door closing and then
count while her car rolls down the driveway and takes off
for Park Street Elementary.

. . . *After they reduced the green pills and orange*
pills because I was such a very, very good little girl, the
fog thinned in my head and my brain shifted back into
DRIVE. Life in jenniferland took a little getting used to.
There were always people around, for one thing. Jennifer
had friends. Dad threw barbecues. Emma suckered them
into letting me babysit her, except for the mornings I had
to go to summer school.

My father ("one hundred and ten, kiddo—you look
great!") bought me a new car ("three years old, eighty

thousand miles, but new tires and very safe") so I could drive Emma to the pool and soccer and her friends' houses. It wasn't like I had anywhere else to go. Cassie had dumped me. My other friends had faded away when I wasn't paying attention. Dad promised me a bunch of road trips to make me feel better. We were going to watch the sunrise over the ocean, listen to the Boston Pops, drive up to Canada for a cup of coffee and turn around and drive home. He was so convincing, I really believed him for a while. But then his editor refused to change his book deadline again and he had to take over a summer session class and we never went anywhere.

My car took me to a medical-supply store where I bought a killer-accurate digital scale. One that could not be tampered with, *unlike the Blubber-O-Meter 3000 . . .*

I remove the real scale from its hiding place in my closet and carry it back to the bathroom. Weight must be measured on a hard surface. The phones ring, one in every room in the house, ding-dong caroling bells. The answering machine picks up.

I pee out the extra water inside me and strip. I stand five feet, five inches tall, a little shorter than freshman year. That's when my periods stopped, too. I pretend to be a fat, healthy teenager. They pretend to be my parents. ~~Everything is just fine.~~

I close my eyes.

As I step on the scale, Jennifer warns Emma about ice cream.

As I step on the scale, Emma fears vanilla.

As I step on the scale, Dad swings his racket and scores.

As I step on the scale, Mom slices open a stranger.

As I step on the scale, shadows edge closer.

As I step on the scale, Cassie dreams.

I open my eyes. 099.00 pounds. I am officially standing on Goal Number One.

Ha.

If my docs knew, they'd bodyslam me back into treatment. There would be consequences and repercussions because (once again) I broke the rules about the perfectsized Lia. I am supposed to be as big as they want. I am supposed to repeat my affirmations like incantations to drive the nasty voices out of my head. I am supposed to commit to recovery like a nun pledging body and soul in a convent.

They are morons. This body has a different metabolism. This body hates dragging around the chains they wrap around it. Proof? At 099.00 I think clearer, look better, feel stronger. When I reach the next goal, it will be all that, and more.

Goal Number Two is 095.00, the perfect point of balance. At 095.00, I will be pure. Light enough to walk with my head up, meaty enough to fool everyone. At 095.00, I will have the strength to stay in control. I'll stand on the blocks hidden in the toes of my satin ballet slippers, pink ribbons sewn into my calves, and rise above up in the air: magical.

At 090.00, I will soar. That's Goal Number Three.

Cassie watches, half hidden in the shower curtain.
"Give it up," she whispers.

◀ **014.00** ▶

I'm late again, and dreaming halfway out the door (099.00! 099.00! 099.00! Tomorrow will be 098.00!) when the red blinking light catches me. The answering machine. Not my problem. Jennifer will get it when she comes home.

But what if it *is* Jennifer, asking me to pick up Emma after school again? Or my dad, needing some important papers he forgot. Or Cassie —

Well, no. Not Cassie.

I set my backpack on the floor, cross back across the frozen kitchen, and press PLAY.

"Um, hello? I hope this is the right number."

A guy's voice. Deep. Nobody I know.

He coughs once. "I'm looking for somebody named Lia. Um, Lia, if this your house, well, duh, if it isn't your house, you won't be getting the message, will you? Can you call the Gateway Motel, or stop by if it's close? Ask for me, Elijah. I promised Cassie I'd—"

The machine cuts off his voice.

I put on one of Dad's extra-large sweatshirts because I can't stop shaking. I listen to the message a dozen times before I call the school nurse and tell her I'm having a really bad day and I'm on my way to an emergency appointment with my shrink. She says she'll tell the office.

I grab my keys.

◀ 015.00 ▶

I drive past front yards trapped between holidays, some with inflatable turkeys on the lawn, others with fake snowmen and high-class wreaths on the front door. Every mailbox has a security-system sign nailed to it. This neighborhood isn't as expensive as the one where Cassie and me grew up, but it tries harder.

The car steers us down to the bypass. I know I'm going to get lost. I always get lost. I should have printed out the directions.

Who is this guy and how did he get my number and is this a scam and should I call the police?

I turn the heat up to ROAST. The first exit takes me to

a bunch of stumpy office buildings with half-empty parking lots. I backtrack to 101. The next exit would take me to the college and, with my luck, I'd run right into my father or one of his scheming grad students.

Third exit: River Road. Turn right. The first blocks are dotted with family stores: a nail salon, a discount-discount store, a diner, mattress store, karate school, furniture rental. At the Laundromat, a little kid with a bottle hanging out of his mouth stands on a chair with both hands on the plate-glass window. He smiles and the bottle falls out. Behind him, a woman dumps clothes from a black garbage bag into a washer.

I roll out of the badlands, past scrub cedar trees and a boarded-up church. Couple of miles later—click on the turn signal, check the mirrors—I turn left into the lot of the Gateway Motel. There are plenty of places to park.

The building reminds me of Emma's shoe-box diorama. Holes are cut out every couple of feet: fat holes for windows, skinny holes for doors. The peeling stucco walls are stained with rust from the dripping gutters. The office is at the far end, a red neon sign blinking in the window: VACA CY.

I get out of the car, lock the door, and head for the office, avoiding the half-feathered carcass of a bird.

◀ 016.00 ▶

It's as cold in the lobby as it is outside. The registration desk has a boot-sized hole in it. Behind it sits an old man with a bad comb-over and thick glasses, reading the newspaper. The small TV attached to the wall has a jumpy picture and no sound. A scarred pay phone is mounted above a rack with a few faded tourist brochures for Canobie Lake Park, Robert Frost Farm, and the New Hampshire Snowmobile Museum. There is a door marked PRIVATE and one that says RESTROOM—GUESTS ONLY.

I shouldn't be here. I should be in Trig. No, History. I should get back in that car and drive to school, slowing down in crosswalks and stopping at yellow lights. Obeying all posted speed limits.

"Yeah?" The man looks up at me and squints. "You want a room?"

I shake my head. "No, sir."

"Well, what do you want?" His voice is wet with tar. "Come to see where she died?" Not the voice from the answering machine.

I give a tiny nod.

"Ten bucks for a peek." He holds out his hand and flips his fingers toward his palm.

I open my wallet. "I only have a five."

"That'll do." After I hand over the bill, he shouts, "Lie-juh!"

The restroom door opens. The guy who steps out looks a couple of years older than me, and is almost a foot taller, with thick black hair to his shoulders and black-rimmed glasses. His skin is sugar-white and, under a lame beard, his face is broken out like a lava field. He's wearing steel-toed boots, baggy black work pants, and a Patriots sweatshirt with a rip in the collar. His eyes are the color of smoke and ringed with thick eyeliner. A brown wooden plug fills up his left earlobe.

He waves the silver wrench in his hand and grins. "You rang, Your Slimeship?"

That's the voice.

"She wants to see it," the older man says, sticking my money in his pocket. "Show her."

The cocky attitude drains away, and his smile vanishes. He sets the wrench on the counter and mumbles, "Follow me."

As I leave, the old man calls out, "Don't be stealing nothing. That's all motel property."

We walk past metal doors, 103, 105, 107. 109 is missing the doorknob. 111 is tagged with black spray paint, but I can't figure out what it says.

The guy stops so suddenly in front of room 113 that I crash into his back.

"Sorry."

"No worries." He unhooks a heavy ring of keys from his belt loop, shaking his head. "You here on a bet?"

"Excuse me?"

"A kid came by an hour ago." He keeps his eyes on his hands, flipping through the keys. "His buddies dared him."

He holds a key between his thumb and first finger, letting the others slide down the ring. "He wanted to see if there was blood."

Brown leaves scuttle past us. The wind blows my hair in my face. I tuck it behind my ears. "Were you here . . . ?"

He sticks the key in the lock, his back to me, voice flat as a museum guide's. "I had the night off. Watched basketball at a bar downtown, then went to a guy's house to play poker. Won eighty bucks. Gave me a hell of an alibi." The door squeaks as he pushes it open. "They figured out what killed her yet?"

I shake my head. "I don't think so."

The wind gusts again. "I hope it was quick."

The room behind him is filled with dark. I shiver. That is the last door Cassie walked through. She walked in alive and she walked out dead.

I shouldn't have come here.

"You have a name?" he asks.

"What? Me?" I shiver so hard my teeth rattle. I don't know this guy and I don't know why he wants to talk to me. "Yeah, um, I'm Emma. You?"

"Elijah."

I wrap my arms around myself. "Was she upset when she checked in?"

He shakes his head. "Didn't see her until it was too late. I live in 115. When I came back after the poker game, I found the door open and the lights on. I found her."

I spin away from him, squeezing my eyes shut. Everything in my body hurts, like I have the flu, or the air seeping out of room 113 infected me with something. My heart slams against its bone cage, over and over, blood seeping down to the cracks in the ground.

"I checked for a pulse," he continues. "Called 911."

"Stop it," I whisper.

He regurgitates his chewed story for me, another paying customer feasting on the dead blonde. Step right up to the freak show, make a video with your phone, blog the blood. Tighten the wire noose hiding under your collarbones.

I open my eyes and turn back around. He's inside, in the shadows, reaching for the light on the dresser.

"I said stop it," I say loudly. "I don't want to see any more." I walk away, legs shaking. "I have to go now."

"Hey," he calls after me. "Come back."

I hum to myself to drown out his voice.

"Hey!" he shouts. "Do you know a girl named Lia?"

I stop, hand on the car door. "What?"

He jogs up to me, stopping a few steps in front of the dead bird. "I'm looking for somebody named Lia. She might go to your school."

"Why?"

He crosses his arms over his chest and shivers once.

The wind has shifted to the north. "I'm just trying to find her."

The bird flutters its wings, bones rattling like dice.

"Sorry," I say. "Never heard of her."

◀ 017.00 ▶

The movie theater is empty except for me in the back row and three ~~nannies~~ moms with sticky kids up front. The projector's light traps a galaxy of swirling skin flakes and popcorn husks in the air. Anime shape-shifters battle bad guys on the screen, a cheap Japanimation matinee.

I open the bag from the drugstore.

Two of the ~~nannies~~ moms talk to each other, while the third argues on her cell. The kids bounce up and down on the seats. Above them, robot monsters are destroying a village. The big-eyed heroes turn into fox-people who shoot fire from their paws.

I take the box of razor blades out of the bag.

::Stupid/ugly/stupid/bitch/stupid/fat/
stupid/baby/stupid/loser/stupid/lost::

A purple robot monster throws a truck at a fox-boy. The speakers vibrate thunderechoes when the truck crashes into the ground. The kids in the audience aren't even watching. They're fighting about their popcorn and candy, and whining about going to the potty.

The box opens and the razors slide out, whisper sweet.

Used to be that my whole body was my canvas—hot cuts licking my ribs, ladder rungs climbing my arms, thick milkweed stalks shooting up my thighs. When I moved to jenniferland, my father made one condition. A daughter who forgets how to eat, well that was bad, but it was just a phase and I was over it. But a daughter who opens her own skin bag, wanting to let her shell fall to the ground so she can dance? That was just sick. No cutting, Lia Marrigan Overbrook. Not under Daddy's roof. Bottom line. Deal breaker.

The fox-heroes on the big screen turn their eyes into lightning. They grit their teeth and wince when the monsters throw them against the mountain, but they always, always get back up, retie their red scarves and laugh.

All of the badness boils under my skin, stingy gingerale bubbles fighting to breathe. I unbutton my jeans, sliding the zipper open one tooth at a time. I twist to the right and push down the elastic band of my underpants. My left hip arches up, glowing blue in the movie light.

::Stupid/ugly/stupid/bitch/stupid/fat/
stupid/baby/stupid/loser/stupid/lost::

I inscribe three lines, *hush hush hush*, into my skin. Ghosts trickle out.

The shape-shifters put on jet packs and follow the

monsters to an asteroid. A ~~nanny~~ mom drags the kid who has to pee to the lobby.

I put the blade back in the box, and the box back in the bag and press my hand against the wet cuts until the credits roll. Just before the lights come up, I stick my fingers in my mouth.

I taste like dirty quarters.

◀ 018.00 ▶

After a day lost in a nightmare, the car takes me away from the movie theater, the drugstore, and the motel that grinds up girls into bite-sized pieces. We roll back to the highway and into the hills, climbing up to the McSame houses of Castle Pines, back to the house of my father set in the clouds.

The three of them are sitting around the dining room table, candles jumping to the harpsichord music drifting from the speakers. The air is damp with dinner—leftover turkey, stinky Brussels sprouts, salad, whole grain rolls, and cheesy potatoes, Emma's favorite. A family meal to remind us that we are a family. We are not a reality show (yet), or strangers sharing a house and splitting the bills. We are not a motel.

There is an empty place across the table from Emma—plate, paper napkin, stainless-steel fork, knife, spoon. Mom got the good silver when my parents split up.

It came from Nanna Marrigan, who said that food served with cheap utensils tasted tinny. She was right.

Daddy looks up, a piece of turkey dangling from his fork. "You're late, kiddo. Have a seat."

"I stayed after to work on a project. Can I eat upstairs? I'm buried with homework."

Emma bounces in her chair. "I made the potatoes, Lia. Almost by myself."

Jennifer nods. "Please, Lia. It's been a while since we had a nice dinner."

My stomach tightens. There is no room inside of me for this.

"I used the peeler and a knife." Emma grins so hard the glass drops hanging from the chandelier shake. "Mommy shredded."

"That's awesome." I pull out my chair and sit. "If you made them, they've got to taste good."

Dad swallows and winks at me.

"Can I have the salad?" I ask.

He passes me the casserole dish filled with gravy and leftover turkey. I have to use both hands to hold it because it weighs more than everything on the table plus the table itself, plus the chandelier and the custom-built cabinet that holds Jennifer's collection of glass figurines.

I set the dish next to my plate. The triangle DadEmma-Jennifer locks in on my hand reaching for the fork. I pull out a full-fat slice of baked flesh, gravy-blooded (250), and let it fall on to my plate. *Splat.*

I hold out the dish to Jennifer. "Want another piece?"

She sets it in the middle of the table and steers the conversation back to Emma's problems with long division.

Dad doesn't even try to hide the fact that he's staring at my plate.

I take a whole wheat roll (96) out of the basket and two buttery Brussels sprouts (35), even though I hate them. In jenniferland I am An Example and must take at least two bites of everything. I set the roll on the edge of the plate, Brussels sprouts at two and four o'clock, equidistant. I stand up so I can reach the cheesy potatoes and plop a disgusting orange spoonful (70) next to the turkey.

Just because I dish it out, doesn't mean I have to swallow it. I am strong enough to do this ~~the potatoes smell so good~~ stay strong, empty empty ~~the potatoes smell~~ strong/empty/strong/breathe/pretend/hold on.

I fill the rest of the space with salad, taking extra mushrooms and leaving the olives in the bowl. Five mushrooms = 20. Eat five magic mushrooms and drink a tall glass of water and they bloom in your belly like fog-colored sponges.

Strong/empty/strong.

Jennifer asks Emma what forty-eight divided by eight equals. Emma bites her roll. Dad nods at my full plate and says he'll quiz Emma after dessert. "Even history profs have to know how to multiply and divide, Emmakins."

I spread my napkin in my lap, then cut my turkey into two pieces, then four, then eight, then sixteen white bites. The Brussels sprouts are quartered. I scrape the cheese off a sliver of potato—which will not kill me, potatoes rarely cause death—and shove it in my mouth and chew, chew, chew, smiling across the acres of tablecloth. Dad and Jennifer watch the division on my plate, but they don't say anything about it. When I first moved in, this would have been called "disordered behavior" and Jennifer's voice would pitch up high and Dad would twist his wedding band around and around his finger. Now it falls under the category of "battles not worth fighting, because at least she's sitting at the table eating with us, and her weight hasn't dropped into dangerland."

I drop my left hand to my lap, under the napkin, under my waistband, and find the three scabby lines, drawn straight and true. With every bite I press my fingers into the cuts.

"You did a great job," I tell Emma. "The potatoes are amazing."

As Dad complains about a professor from Chicago who just published a book that is exactly like the one that Dad is writing, I skate the food from the one o'clock position to the two, then the three o'clock edge of my plate. I squeeze the gravy through the tines of my fork.

Jennifer asks Emma to divide one-hundred-twenty-one by eleven. Emma can't.

I chew every bite ten times before I swallow. Meat in my mouth, chew ten times, lettuce in my mouth, chew chew chew chew chew chew chew chew chew chew, soggy

Brussels sprout, mushroom cap, chew, chew, chew. I sip the milk, staining my top lip white and proving that we are all just fine.

"Can you figure out one hundred divided by ten?" asks Jennifer.

A tear rolls down Emma's cheek and splashes on her cheesy potatoes.

Dad pauses his rant and holds up his hands. "No tears, Emma. Lia had a hard time memorizing this stuff, too, but she got it in the end."

That's my cue. "You know what saved me?" I ask. "Calculators. As long as you have a calculator, you'll be okay. Trust me, math is not worth crying about."

Jennifer shoots me a steplook, sharper than normal, and pours another glass of water. "Didn't you have a test today?"

I spear the thinnest slice of potato. "Physics. He postponed it. Nobody understands the speed of light. How's the migraine?"

"Like a herd of cattle stampeding through my head."

"Ouch," I say. Emma tries to cut a Brussels sprout with her fork, but it jumps off her plate and rolls across the table to me. Jennifer winces when the fork screeches across the plate. I toss the runaway sprout to Emma, who catches it with a giggle and wipes her eyes on her sleeve.

Jennifer reaches over to take the sprout out of Emma's hand, and knocks over the glass of milk. Emma flinches as the milk floods her plate, then soaks the tablecloth and starts to drip on the new carpet.

The phone rings. Jennifer buries her head in her hands.

Dad stands up. "Let the answering machine get it," he says. "I'll clean up the mess."

Jennifer takes a deep breath and heads for the kitchen. "I hate people who screen their calls. I'll get it."

Dad mops up the spill, pats Emma's back, and tells her it's just a glass of milk. I sweep my roll and half the meat into my napkin, fold it up and put it in my lap.

Jennifer comes back with her mouth in a perfect knot. "It's her." She holds the phone out to Dad.

Jennifer is not the reason my parents got divorced. The reason was named Amber, and before her Whitney, and before her Jill and the others. When Mom finally kicked him out, Dad went to a new bank to open his own checking account. Jennifer worked there. He was so smitten he went back every day for a week, making up dumb questions about home equity loans and IRAs. They were married before I was used to the fact that my parents had actually divorced.

Dad takes the phone. "Hello? Hang on. . . . Chloe, I can hear you —"

Jennifer frowns and shakes her head.

He gets the message. "We're eating dinner," he says as he walks out, phone three inches from his ear. "Yes, all of us. She's dealing with it fine."

As he walks down the hall the music stops. The CD player *cli-clicks* and changes disks: Tchaikovsky, *Swan Lake*. Jennifer tells Emma to wipe the cheese sauce off her chin.

◀ 019.00 ▶

Half an hour later, Dad opens the door to Mom. Her voice in the hall lashes me to my chair with prickly vines. The last time I saw her was August 31, the day I turned eighteen.

~~I can't see her see me now~~ strong/empty/strong.

The breakup with my mother was the same old story told a million times. Girl is born, girl learns to talk and walk, girl mispronounces words and falls down. Over and over again. Girl forgets to eat, fails adolescence, mother washes her hands of Girl, scrubbing with surgical soap and a brush for three full minutes, then gloving up before handing her over to specialists and telling them to experiment at will. When they let her out, Girl rebels.

Mom walks into the dining room, and Jennifer vanishes, *poof!* It screws up the laws of physics for her to occupy the same room as the first wife.

"Late rounds?" Dad asks.

Mom ignores him and walks toward me. She kisses

my cheek and pulls back to study me with her X-ray/MRI/CAT scan–vision. "How are you feeling?"

"Great," I say.

"I've missed you." She gives me another kiss, lips cool and chapped. When she sits in Jennifer's chair, she winces. Her knees act up when the weather changes.

"You look tired," she says.

"Pot calling the kettle black," I say.

Dr. Chloe Marrigan wears her fatigue like a suit of armor. To be the best, you have to give everything all the time, then you have to give some more: hundred-hour weeks, crushing patient loads, working miracles the way other people flip burgers. But tonight she looks worse than usual. I don't remember seeing those lines around her mouth. Her corn-yellow hair is tamed into a tight French braid, but a few strands of silver hair flash in the candlelight. The skin on her face used to be tight as a drum. Now it's sagging a little at her neck.

Dad tries to make small talk again. "Was it an emergency surgery?"

She nods. "Quintuple bypass. The guy was a mess."

"Will he make it?" Dad asks.

She puts her pager next to Jennifer's dirty fork. "Doubtful." She measures the three bites of turkey left on my plate and the bread crumbs that I scattered next to it. "Lia looks pale. Has she been eating?"

"Of course she has," Dad says.

It took her seven sentences to piss me off. That's an

Olympic-qualifying accomplishment. I lock my mouth, stand up, pick up my plate, pick up my father's plate, and walk out of the room.

Jennifer and Emma are at the kitchen table, a stack of flash cards between them so the quizzing of division facts can continue. I load the dishwasher as slowly as I can and signal the answers to Emma by drawing numbers in the air behind Jennifer's back.

Dad calls to me from the dining room. "Lia, come back in here, please."

"Good luck," Jennifer murmurs as I leave the room.

"Thanks."

I put Emma's silverware on her plate, but Dad says, "Don't worry about the dishes. We need to talk."

Talk = yell + scold + argue + demand.

Dr. Marrigan pushes up the sleeves of her green silk turtleneck. Her nails are short and polish-free, the magic fingers connected to the hands connected to the forearms roped with steel muscle and tendons that lead to shoulders, neck, and bionic brain. Her fingertips drum the table. "Sit down, please," she says.

I sit.

Daddy: Your mother has a concern.

Mom: It's more than a concern.

Lia: About?

Daddy: I told her that you've been fine since we got the news.

Lia: He's right.

Mom, spine not touching the back of her chair: I'm afraid Cassie's death might trigger you. The research shows—

Lia: I'm not a lab rat.

Mom glances at the blank screen of her pager, hoping it will go off.

Lia: We stopped talking months ago.

Mom: You were best friends for nine years. Not talking for a couple months doesn't make that go away.

Lia stares at a stain in the tablecloth.

Daddy: Do you know how she died?

Mom, taking a roll from the basket: Cindy will call me when the autopsy results come in. I offered to explain them to her.

Daddy: I bet it will show drugs.

Mom: Maybe, but that's not the point. The point is Lia.

Emma walks in to say good night, her eyes puffy. Dad kisses her; Dr. Marrigan gives her a clinical smile. I hug her close and whisper that long division is a stupid poophead. She giggles and squeezes me tight, then runs up to take her bath. Jennifer stands with her back to Dr. Marrigan and me and asks her husband some lame questions about the garbage pickup tomorrow and his socks in the dryer, little homey details to remind Wife Number One who wears the diamond ring around here.

I brush the crumbs from the tablecloth into my hand. Drugs didn't kill Cassie, not unless it was a couple of bottles of aspirin. Or she drank vodka until she fell into a coma. Or she cut too deep. Or maybe someone else killed her, some bad guy who followed her and stole her purse and emptied her checking account.

No, that would have been in the newspaper.

I should have asked Elijah what he saw, what the police really said. I should have told him my name. But, no. I don't know who he is, not really. What if he lied about having an alibi, what if the police think he's a suspect? And what kind of guy lives in a creepy motel? Maybe he was a figment of my imagination. The whole day could have been a blackout dream I spun for myself because admitting that I spent the whole day in bed is pathetic.

Doubtful.

Poof! Jennifer vanishes again.

Mom, taking roll out of basket: I can't go to the wake because of work. Are you going?

Dad: It might be awkward. I haven't talked to them in years.

Lia: I'll go.

Mom: Absolutely not. You're emotionally fragile. I'll pay our respects at the funeral on Saturday.

Lia: But you just made a big deal about how long Cassie and me were friends.

Dad: Your mother is right. It'll upset you too much.

Lia: I'm not upset.

Mom: I don't believe you. I want you to see Dr. Parker more frequently. At least once a week, maybe more.

Lia, quietly: No. It's a waste of time and money.

Dad: What do you mean?

Lia: Dr. Parker is dragging out my therapy so she can keep getting paid.

Mom, picking out bits of grain from roll: You're alive because of Dr. Parker.

Lia, bleeding where they can't see: Stop exaggerating.

Mom, dropping crumbs: She's slipping back into denial, David. Why are you letting this happen? You're not supporting her recovery, you're letting it go up in flames.

Dad: What are you talking about? We're a hundred percent supportive, aren't we, Lia?

Mom, acid-eyes: You coddle her, you let her call the shots.

Dad, louder: Did you just say we coddle her?

They leap into battle, the steps to the dance burned into their muscle memory. I pull a candle close to me and push the soft wax at the top of it into the blue flame.

My parents met at a midsummer's party by a lake in the mountains. Dad was finishing up his PhD and knew the guy who owned the cabin. Mom had a rare night off between her internship and residency. She and her friends were looking for a different party and got lost.

When I was a real girl, they would cuddle with me on the couch and tell me the fairy-tale version of how they fell in love:

Once upon a time, on the shores of a purple lake so deep it had no bottom, a man saw a lady with long golden hair walking barefoot in the sand. The lady heard the man singing sweetly and playing the guitar. It was fate that their paths should cross.

They paddled a canoe to the middle of the water and laughed. The moon saw how beautiful they were and how much in love, and gave them a baby for their very own. Just then, the canoe sprung a leak and started to sink. They had to paddle hard, hard, hard, but they made it to shore just in time.

They named the baby Lia and lived happily ever after.

The skin on the edge of my thumb rests on the cusp between safety and flame.

The real story is not poetic. Mom got pregnant. Dad married her. They couldn't stand each other by the time I was born. They were random gods who mated by a wine-dark sea. They should have turned me into a fish or a flower when they had the chance.

Mom: She looks like hell. I want her to move back with me until she graduates.

Dad, throwing napkin on table: Oh, for Christ's sake, Chloe . . .

The two of them will fight forever.
I blow out the candle.

Emma hears me come up the stairs and asks me to watch a movie with her. I stick Band-Aids on my weeping cuts, put on pink pajamas so we match, and snuggle with her under her rainbow comforter. She arranges all of her stuffed animals around us in a circle, everyone facing the TV, then presses PLAY.

When she falls asleep, I flip through the channels one after the other after the other.

Dr. Marrigan leaves an hour later, without bothering to come up and say good night or notice that I haven't unpacked most of my boxes or see what a good almost-sister I can be. The front door closes hard with a muffled *whoomp* that pushes air against all the windows. Professor Overbrook bolts the door and sets the security system. I turn out the princess light next to the bed. Emma breathes through her open mouth.

Ghosts dare not enter here. I fall asleep with my head on a raggedy elephant.

◀ 020.00 ▶

"Wake up, Lia!" Emma shouts in my ear. "You're going to be late! You're going to be in trouble."

I'm under Emma's tie-dyed comforter, my head on the elephant. Her room smells like dryer sheets and cats.

"Don't go back to sleep again!"

"What day is it?" I ask.

"You know," she says.

Today is waking Wednesday.

History class is a genocide lecture, ending with ten minutes of photographs of Polish children killed by the Germans in World War II. A couple of girls cry and the guys who usually make smart-ass remarks stare out the windows. Our Trig teacher is deeply, deeply disappointed in our last test results. We have another ~~nap~~ movie in Physics: *An Introduction to Momentum and Collision.* My English teacher flips out because the government is demanding we take yet another test to assess our reading skills, because we're seniors and pretty soon we might have to read or something.

I eat in my car: diet soda (0) + lettuce (15) + 8 tablespoons salsa (40) + hard-boiled egg white (16) = lunch (71).

※ ※ ※

Two minutes before the buzzer sounds to set us free at the end of the day, the loudspeaker orders me to see the counselor, Ms. Rostoff, in the conference room. Most of the girls' soccer team is there, too, along with Cassie's friends from the stage crew and a couple of girls from the musical. Mira, my study partner from sophomore Spanish, waves to me when I walk in. She was in our Girl Scout troop when we were little.

We are here to share our feelings and discuss a memorial to Cassie's memory, "so her spirit will live on." The room is freezing.

Ms. Rostoff has boxes of tissues decorated with kittens lined up on the table. Two gallons of discount-store red punch and tiny paper cups are arranged in a lovely display next to the plate of generic black-and-white cookies. Ms. Rostoff believes in the healing power of snacks. She loves me better than anybody because I am such a mess I have to see a real shrink in the real world, and I have to go to the college where my dad teaches, so advising me took two minutes.

The drama girls take over the beat-up couch and the rug in front of it. The soccer team wheels in spinny chairs from the conference room. I sit on the floor near the door, my back against the heating vent.

While we wait for stragglers, the soccer team complains about not getting enough time in the weight room, and the drama girls whine about the new director, a prima donna who has confused our school with Broadway. I measure myself; I can't act or play soccer, and most of them have better grades than me. But I am the thinnest girl in the room, hands down.

There is an awkward pause between stories and the room gets too quiet. Someone farts softly. The heat comes on.

I don't know how they do it. I don't know how anybody does it, waking up every morning and eating and moving from the bus to the assembly line, where the teacher-bots inject us with Subject A and Subject B, and passing every test they give us. Our parents provide the list of ingredients and remind us to make healthy choices: one sport, two clubs, one artistic goal, community service, no grades below a B, because really, nobody's average, not around here. It's a dance with complicated footwork and a changing tempo.

I'm the girl who trips on the dance floor and can't find her way to the exit. All eyes on me.

Ms. Rostoff looks at her watch. It keeps better time than the clock on the wall. "All right, girls."

A drama raises her hand—BMI 20. Maybe 19.5. Her sneakers are painted, one with an impossibly small checkerboard of a thousand colors, the other with yellow happy faces alternating with black skulls. "Ms. Rostoff? Can we have a moment of silence?"

Ms. Rostoff calculates. Will our parents scream at the

school board if she allows a religious ritual in her office? Or will they scream if she denies us our freedom of religious expression?

"Is everyone interested in that?"

We nod, the strings attached to our heads twitching.

"Okay then." She looks at her watch again. "A moment for Cassie."

Drama and soccer bow their heads. I do, too. I am supposed to pray, I think. I can never tell with moments of silence. They're so . . . silent. Empty.

Somebody sniffs and pulls a tissue from the box. I peek out through my eyelashes. Mira's eyes are closed tight and her lips are moving. A girl I've never seen before wipes her face with a dirty Kleenex from her pocket. A soccer player pulls out her phone to read a text. Ms. Rostoff rubs her artificial nails against her thumb, then checks her watch again.

"Thank you, everyone."

She ~~proclaims the rules~~ establishes the parameters of our discussion. We will not talk about how Cassie died, or why, or where, or who in this room could have done something to stop her or at least slow her down. We're here to celebrate her life.

thirty-three calls.

Ms. Rostoff has already arranged for a memorial page in the yearbook, and she wrote an obituary for the school newspaper. The soccer team says they are dedicating the rest of their season to Cassie, both weeks of it. The theater girls want to take a moment just before the musical starts, when the houselights go out and the stage is black, to light up a single rose in a vase at the center of the stage while the chorus sings "Amazing Grace," and then the star of the play will read a poem about the tragedy of dying too soon.

The idea gets trimmed down to the rose in the spotlight for a minute and a mention in the play bulletin.

"What about Lia?" Mira leans forward to see me better. "Do you want to do something special? You guys were best friends."

Were.

"These are all great ideas," my lips say. "But I think Ms. Rostoff should talk to Cassie's parents. Get their opinion."

Diversion successful. The counselor talks about the family's loss and how we can support them and how we have to be there for each other and how her door is always open and the tissue boxes always full. Before we leave, the soccer captain reminds the team to wear their uniforms to tonight's wake. Mira says everyone from the play will go in black.

◀ 021.00 ▶

I am wearing navy blue tights under a stained pair of baggy jeans, a long underwear shirt, a turtleneck, a hoodie sweatshirt I stole from my father's closet, and my jacket, with a surprise for Cassie buried deep in the left pocket. And mittens. Not what you wear to a wake.

I tell Jennifer I won't be home for dinner because I have to do research at the library with stupid primary sources, which means I have to use an actual book that has probably been touched by a hundred thousand strangers carrying God knows what mutant strains of virus.

It is such a bad lie I'm sure she'll bust me for it, but she's up to her elbows in papier-mâché helping Emma make a Greek temple.

My car parks at the library. I hurry the two blocks to the church, keeping my head down and my hair in my face. The sun set an hour ago. Cold air blows in with the smell of burning leaves and dead things piled onto bonfires. Red-and-green Christmas decorations are hung on the streetlights and in all the stores.

I can feel the shadows slipping out of the dark, coming for me.

Last time I was locked up, the hospital shrink had me draw a life-sized outline of my body. I chose a fat crayon the color of elephant skin or a rainy sidewalk. He unrolled the paper on the floor, butcher's paper that crinkled when I leaned on it. I wanted to draw my thighs, each the size of a couch, on his carpet. The rolls on my butt and my gut would rumble over the floor and splash up against the walls; my boobs, beach balls; my arms, tubes of cookie dough oozing at the seams.

The doc would have been horrified. All his work, gone, in the endless loop of snot-gray crayon. He would have called my parents and there would be more consultations (meter running, thousands of insurance dollars ticking away), and he would have adjusted my meds again, one pill to make my self-of-steam larger, another to make my craziness small.

So I drew a blobby version of me, a fraction of my real size, fingers and toes accounted for, stones in my belly, cute earrings, ponytail.

He pulled another long sheet of paper from the roll and had me lay down on it so he could draw the outside of me, life-sized. The crayon hugged my bones tight and it made me shiver. He did not dare approach my inner thighs. He did not speculate about the size or condition of my interior organs.

I pulled a magazine off the table while he taped the drawings to the wall. It was a trigger magazine, strategically placed to send sparks into the air that could catch fire and burn clean away the craziness of his ~~patience~~ patients.

Even the ugly people in the magazine were beautiful.

"Look up here," he said. "What differences do you see, Lia?"

Truth? They were both hideous waxy ghosts on butcher paper. I knew what he wanted to hear. He couldn't stand me being sick. Nobody can. They only want to hear that you're healing, you're in recovery, taking it one day at a time. If you're locked into sick, you should stop wasting their time and just get dead.

"Lia?" he asked again.

The $$$$ were ticking away.

I recited my lines. "The picture I drew is bloated and unrealistic. I guess I have to work on my self-perception a little more."

He smiled.

I had figured out that my eyes were broken long before that. But that day *I started to worry that the people in charge couldn't see, either.*

I stop in front of the florist shop. On the second floor, the lights are on in my old dance studio. I spent a lifetime staring into the mirrors up there. I'd flex and leap, and bow and sweep; a sugarplum, a swan, a maiden, a doll. After rehearsal I'd steal my mother's anatomy book and stand naked in the bathroom, tracing the muscles that swam under my skin, looking for the place where they thinned into tough tendon ribbons anchored in the bones.

The girl reflected back from the window in front of me has poinsettias growing out of her belly and head. She's the shape of a breakfast-link sausage standing on broomstick legs, her arms made from twigs, her face blurred with an eraser. I know that it is me, but it's not me, not really. I don't know what I look like. I can't remember how to look.

Gray faces crowd the red leaves. The ghosts want to taste me. Their hands snake out, fingers open wide. I walk quickly, moving out of the reach of their sticky shadows. As I pass under a streetlight, the bulb pops and I smell burnt sugar. Her. *Her.*

I run the rest of the way to the wake, one step ahead of the iron hooks she's casting.

◂   022.00   ▸

The line of people waiting to stare at the empty body snakes out the front door of the church and down the steps to the sidewalk. Dark chords from the organ slip into the night, turning our shoes into concrete blocks and pulling down our faces until we look like trees drooping with black leaves.

We've all been here before. In fifth grade it was Jimmy Myers, leukemia. In eighth, Madison Ellerson and her parents died in a thirty-car pileup during a blizzard. Last year it was a guy from the tennis team, the one who made State. Didn't buckle his seat belt, no airbags. When his car hit a truck, he launched through the windshield in a perfect arc until he landed, tangled and speared, in the arms of a pine tree. The line for his wake went all the way around the block.

Walking through the front door, I am hit by the buzz of people talking but trying not to be heard. Parents unbutton their coats and drape them awkwardly over their arms. Sweat beads up on the cheeks of boys, leaning on the walls with their hands in their pockets and their ties loosened. Girls teeter-totter on their highest heels and thank God it is not them in the pretty box up front.

I leave my jacket on, unzipped. For the first time in weeks, I am almost warm. Plastic candles with orange bulbs flicker along the dark windows. The line moves along at a steady pace, like we're filing in to a concert or a football game. When the soccer team walks by the casket, the captain hands a team ball signed by all the girls to Cassie's father. He gives it to a man in black who puts the offering in with the corpse, gently, so she doesn't wake up.

It's called a wake, but nobody really wants the dead to rise.

The closer I get to the coffin, the hotter it is. Brown-edged chrysanthemum petals drop loudly from the wreaths that are perched on metal holders. I'm wilting, too, and my head is filling with rusty nails. I shouldn't have worn jeans. *Idiot.*

There is a gap between me and the guy ahead of me, a space big enough for four people. A lady behind me hisses, "Move up."

Suddenly the organist stops playing. People stop in mid-murmur. The organist reaches for something above her and a whole stack of books falls to the floor, echoing across the marble like a gunshot. People jump.

I can see the bottom of the box now. The soccer ball rests next to a folded black T-shirt from the stage crew. Cassie's feet are hidden under a white velvet sheet, toes sticking straight up. I hope they put warm slippers on her, and comfy socks. I hope they left on her toe ring.

The music starts up again, a long, trembling minor chord.

The guy in front of me walks over to Cassie's parents. Her mother sobs and he puts his arms around her. He's an uncle, the fun one, the one who taught us how to water-ski. He is crying, too, groaning. They are the only two people in this whole hot, crowded, dead-petal church strong enough to say and do what we are all thinking.

My turn to stare. My turn to rape the dead.

Sleeping Beauty is wearing a sky blue dress with a high neck and long sleeves. Her hair looks like an over-brushed doll's wig, tired yellow with faded red highlights coming through. She is not wearing any earrings or her silver bell necklace, but her class ring was shoved on her finger. Her nose piercing and acne scars are hidden under the foundation plastered on her skin. They used the wrong shade of pale.

I want to take off her dress and see if they unzipped her belly. I want to look inside. She would, too, because that's all we ever talked about, the hidden creatures with itchy wings and antennae that poked us and sent us stumbling to the bathroom, Cassie to the toilet so she could get rid of it all, me to the mirror so the girl on the other side would keep me strong and steel-ribbed.

They should have put her crochet needle in the box next to her, and yarn so she'll have something to do in Eternity. Some Gaiman, Tolkien, Butler, a few tabloids, mints—peppermint, not wintergreen—her swimming ribbons and Girl Scout badges, the posters from the plays she was in. I bet she'd like a box of cereal to munch on, too: comfort food for the ride.

Her mother sobs louder than the organ.

I reach into my jacket pocket and pull out the small disk of green see-glass, born in the heart of a volcano, capable of showing the future. I stole it from Cassie's room when we were nine, but I could never make it work, no matter how the stars lined up.

I slip the magic glass into her frozen hand.

Cassie's fingers curl around it.

My heart stutters.

She squeezes the green disk tightly, then she blinks—

once, twice—opens her eyes wide, and looks straight at me. She reaches up and touches her hair. It comes out of her head like dandelion fluff. A few strands float up to the real candles burning at the head of the box. They ignite like sparklers.

I cannot breathe.

Cassie sits up slowly. She holds the magic glass up to her blue eye, looks through it and laughs, a low, dirty sound that only came out at two or three o'clock in the morning. She pops the glass in her mouth and swallows it, then wipes her mouth with her hand, staining her fingers with wax and blood.

She frowns and opens her mouth—

—no. She is not sitting there. She's not there at all. There is no blood, no cloud of doll hair burning up in the candle fire.

I blink. She has disappeared from the coffin. The soccer ball rolls backwards. Her feet aren't there to prop it up.

I blink.

She's still gone, the white velvet sheet thrown to the side like she didn't hear the alarm go off and now she's going to be really late and her dad will take the car away again and she'll have to drive with me, and that's a little scary.

The organ music pours down and floods the church.

❋ ❋ ❋

The line behind me mutters. People have places to go and things to do and the new episodes come on in half an hour, and besides, they are all much too polite to notice that the coffin is empty. The fun uncle is buttoning up his coat. The space in front of Cassie's parents waits for me.

A hand touches my shoulder and a guy whispers in my ear. "It's okay. Go on. I'm right behind you."

I trip, then shuffle, eyes down, over to her mom. Mrs. Parrish drapes her arms around me without a word and lays her head on my shoulder. I pat her on the back. Mr. Parrish shakes the hand of the guy behind me and says something that I can't hear because Cassie's mom is so heavy that she is dragging me under the hip-deep water in the sanctuary and down through the marble floor. She wants us to sink below the basement into the warm crawly dirt, where Cassie has a room waiting, so the three of us can curl into critter balls and wait for spring.

The hand touches me again. Mr. Parrish pulls us out of the ground and unpeels his wife from me. He fierce-kisses my forehead, but can't find anything to say.

"We're so sorry for your loss," says the smoke-eyed Elijah guy attached to the hand that is holding mine. "Words aren't enough."

He pulls me into the tide moving out the door. I stumble, and he grabs my arm to keep me from falling.

◀ 023.00 ▶

"Drink this."

Elijah pushes a heavy mug of hot chocolate toward me. I don't remember who ordered it. I don't remember walking here.

"Go on."

I use both hands to pick up the mug, and sip. It burns my lips and tongue and my pink throat. Serves me right. My hands shake as I set the mug back down, and it sloshes on the table. He pulls paper napkins from the metal holder to wipe up the spill.

I know this place, I've been here before. It's the vegetarian diner a couple of blocks from the church, the place with chill music, hemp bagels, and petitions at the cash register.

"How you doing, Emma?" he asks.

It takes a minute to register that he's talking to me, that I still haven't told him who I am because it's easier to lie. I should say "Much better, thanks, how are you?" with the good-girl smile, but I am too freaking tired.

He pushes the soggy napkins to the end of the table. "Seeing dead people can be weird."

I hold my fingers in the steam rising from the mug and watch the cook working the grill, the toaster, and the blender. Cassie is sitting in every chair, laughing, chewing, pointing at the special on the menu.

"She's not in her coffin," I blurt out.

He freezes for a second, eyes fixed on mine. His hair is washed and pulled back into a short ponytail. The wooden plug in his earlobe has been switched out for a hollow bone circle that makes a round window next to his jaw. He's wearing a button-down dingy shirt with a sad black tie. His hands are clean. He shaved, sort of.

"I know," he says. "That's just her shell, not her soul."

I shake my head. "That's not what I mean. She sat up in the coffin. Then she disappeared. Didn't you see that?"

He lays both of his hands on mine and leans forward. They're so warm they should be glowing. "Do me a favor," he says slowly. "Take a sip, close your eyes, and breathe."

"That's dumb."

He smiles and nods. "Yeah, I know. But do it anyway."

My hands raise the mug to my lips again. I am muffled in white velvet sheets. The beads click on my abacus: twelve ounces of hot chocolate = 400, but I am freezing. I need to ~~gulp the whole thing down and ask for more~~ drink one mouthful and ignore the taste.

I sip, set down the mug, no spilling, and close my eyes. Breathe, he said. I breathe in pancakes and french fries. Nervous smells.

"Keep breathing," he orders, his voice a rumble of faraway thunder.

The cook puts something on the griddle and it hisses.

Chair legs scratch the floor as the guy sitting at the table next to us leaves. Someone lifts a rack of glasses that tinkle together like rain. A couple of women laugh, their voices tripping over each other. The bathroom door squeaks.

"Ready?" he asks. "Open your eyes. Don't think. Just open your eyes and be still."

The diner comes back into focus: tables, chairs, lights, kitchen. Posters covering the walls. Through the hole in Elijah's earlobe I can see the crescent moon and stars painted on the wall under the clock. The girl sitting next to it is not Cassie. Neither is the waiter refilling her mug. I turn in my seat to look around. Nobody here is Cassie. I'm safe.

"Better?" he asks.

"Better. Thanks."

"No problem." He spears a forkful of waffle drenched in maple syrup. "You had a shaky moment. It happens." He shovels the waffle into his mouth.

"Wait," I say. "Where did that come from?"

He points to the table next to us. The waitress hasn't cleaned it off. It still has her five-dollar bill stuck under the saltshaker, a half-empty cup of coffee, a dirty fork, and an empty place mat with syrup stains.

"They were just going to throw it away."

"That's disgusting, what about the germs?"

"Free food never makes me sick. You want some?"

"No way."

He laughs so loud that people turn and stare.

"Are you always this strange?"

He laughs again. "Stranger. See this?" He rolls up his sleeve to show the tattoo that takes up his entire forearm: a muscular half-bull, half-man thing riding a bike through a wall of flame, with wings sprouting from its legs and arms and helmet.

"What is that supposed to be?"

"He's the god of bike messengers. Cool, huh? This vision of him came to me one day when I was delivering a package to a law firm in Boston. Saw him so clearly I thought he'd reach out and choke me. He had to go in my skin."

"You have visions."

"It's a gift. You should see the tattoo on my butt."

"No, thanks." I give the diner a quick glance. Still no Cassies. "What if you get a vision you don't like?"

"Doesn't matter if I like it or not. What matters is that I pay attention, and figure out why it was sent to me."

His eyes dart to something over my shoulder, and he suddenly shoves the waffle plate across the table, almost dumping it in my lap.

Our waitress appears, long denim skirt, thick Icelandic sweater, tiny shells dangling from cartilage piercings. BMI 23. She rests the tray on her padded hip and frowns at the waffles. "When did you order those?"

"I didn't," I say.

Elijah gently kicks my leg under the table. "My buddy

gave them to her," he says. "The guy with the beat-up Bruins jacket—he left a couple minutes ago."

She narrows her eyes, smelling a scam. "Are you sure?"

"He didn't stick us with the bill, did he?" Elijah asks.

"No." She shakes her head. "He paid."

"Left you a good tip, too, so no worries, right?" He points to her tray. "Is that mine?"

She sets the plate of toasted brown bread and a small crock of red jam in front of him and walks away without another word.

He dumps the jam on the bread, spreading it thick with the knife.

"Can I ask you a question?"

He takes a bite. "Anything."

"What's a bike messenger with visions doing in the middle of Nowhere, New Hampshire?"

"I don't live in Nowhere, I live in Centerville. Want a bite?"

~~Sure~~ "No." I shake my head. "Not hungry."

"And I *used* to be a bike messenger. Right now I'm a handyman. Turns out I have mad skills with a wrench." He folds the bread in half and stuffs most of it in his mouth. "It's crazy. I can do anything."

"Right. Sure." I laugh and accidentally drink some hot chocolate. "Like what?"

"Where should I start? Poet, philosopher, fisherman.

My pop calls me a bum, but that's elitist, don't you think? I can split wood, spread mulch, pour beer, and grow perfect tomatoes."

"Sure you can."

"I'm an ace poker player, a shaman, and a wanderer in search of truth. I can drive a cab, a motorcycle, and ride a bull, but not for long. I shovel manure in an original and artistic manner. As soon as I get my car fixed up, I will become a gypsy looking for a lost world."

"And you're a thief," I add.

"When the situation calls for it." He pulls the syrupy plate back in front of him and dips the toast in it.

"Why don't you just use your powers to win the lottery or make money grow on trees instead of stealing food?"

"That would be boring." He licks syrup off the side of his hand. "Your turn. What are you?"

"Sad." The word falls out.

"You knew her well, didn't you?"

The lights flicker behind my eyes. I knew her a whole world. I knew her sleepovers and cookie sales and crushes on boybands and the time I broke my leg riding on the back of her bike and the time I helped her paint her room white after she painted it black without permission.

"Tell me something about her," he says. "Something nice."

"She loved waffles."

"Doesn't everybody?"

"She said the world would be a better place if we all used waffles instead of bread."

He eats a spoonful of jam. "Why?"

"Because they taste better and 'waffle' is more fun to say."

"Good point."

The scowly waitress comes by and leaves the check facedown on the table. Elijah flips it over and glances at the total.

I take out my wallet. "What do I owe?"

He reaches in his pocket. "I got it."

"You sure?"

"Yep." He dumps a handful of change by his plate. "But only if you finish that hot chocolate. I cleaned out a septic tank to earn this money. Not that you should feel guilty or anything."

I fight a smile and curl my hand around the mug. ~~I am a healthy teenage girl in a diner, and I can sip a little more hot chocolate. And this feels good and~~ I don't want to go home, not when I'm just starting to warm up. I'll let the skin form on top of hot chocolate and be so grossed out by it, I can't drink any more. He can't expect me to drink skin. I'll stay for twenty minutes, until the library closes. "You still hungry?" I ask.

"Always. The smell of those french fries is killing me."

"Why don't you order some?"

"Can't." He points to the pile of change. "That's all I have on me."

I pull out my debit card and wave it at him. "No problem."

Two french fries = 20.

◀ 024.00 ▶

I am almost a real girl the entire drive home. I went to a diner. I drank hot chocolate and ate french fries. Talked to a guy for a while. Laughed a couple of times. A little like ice-skating for the first time, wobbly, but I did it.

As I walk in the house, the whispers start up again....

... she called.
thirty-three times.
you didn't answer.
body found in a motel room, alone.
you left her alone.
should should should have done anythingeverything.
you killed her.

I try to squeeze them out by focusing loudly. *I am walking up the stairs. I am walking in my room. I am—*

you left her alone.

—shut up, I am throwing my purse on the bed. I am

changing into my pajamas. I need my robe, I think I hung it up—

I open my closet.

you left me alone.

Cassie is leaning against the stack of boxes. She tilts her head to one side and waves. "Have a nice time?"

I slam the door so hard the frame cracks.

She almost went to a doctor two years ago. The stuffing/puking/stuffing/puking/stuffing/puking didn't make her skinny, it made her cry. Her coach bumped her down to the JV soccer squad because she couldn't run fast enough. The drama teacher told her that she wasn't "shining" bright enough so she didn't get the lead in the play.

"I can't stop, but I can't keep going," she told me. "Nothing works."

I totally supported her. I looked up the names of docs and clinics. I e-mailed her recovery Web sites.

And I sabotaged every step.

I told her how strong she was and how healthy she was going to be and how proud I was of her and I dropped in how many calories I ate that day, the magic number on the scale, the number of inches around my thighs. We went to the mall and I made sure we used the same dressing room so she could see my skeleton shine in the fluorescent blue light. We went to the food court and she ordered cheese fries, chicken nuggets, and a salad. I drank black coffee and licked artificial sweetener from the palm on my hand. She asked me to guard the door while she puked lunch into the dirty mall toilet.

We held hands when we walked down the ginger-bread path into the forest, blood dripping from our fingers. We danced with witches and kissed monsters. We turned us into wintergirls, and when she tried to leave, *I pulled her back into the snow because I was afraid to be alone.*

I stay up past midnight reading in the family room in the hopes that Cassie will get bored and go away. Just as I'm ready to head down to the basement ~~to burn away my leg muscles until the sun comes up~~ to exercise moderately for twenty minutes so I'll sleep better, Dad comes clumping down the stairs and into the kitchen. I hear the refrigerator open, then a long spray of whipped cream. The refrigerator closes and he heads my way.

"Lia?" Dad is wearing a blue-and-green-checked robe that is older than me, flannel pajama pants, and a gray T-shirt that says ATHLETIC DEPARTMENT. His feet are bare. His too-long hair, more silver than black, is sticking out all over the place. He looks like a homeless guy begging for change on a corner, but instead of an empty can, he's holding a pie plate buried under a mound of whipped cream. The last two pieces of pumpkin pie from Thanksgiving dinner, I bet.

"What are you doing up?" he asks. "You should be asleep."

I hold up Neil Gaiman's latest work of genius. "I have to see what happens at the end. What about you?"

He carefully sits down in the recliner, pie plate in his lap, and digs in for the first bite. "I keep dreaming about my research and waking up Jennifer because I'm punching the mattress." He frowns. "I should never have agreed to write this one."

"Why not?" I ask.

He takes another bite and chews. ~~The smell curls up next to me, sweet sweet pumpkin, whipped cream melting on my tongue~~ That pie is almost a week old, slick mold is growing in the crust, it'll make him sick.

He wipes a dab of whipped cream from his mouth. "I didn't do enough preliminary research before I wrote the proposal. I assumed that I'd find plenty of primary sources and made too many promises. Now I'm stuck."

"Tell your editor," I say. "Tell her you made a mistake and offer to write a different book."

"It's not that simple." He shovels in another enormous hunk of pie.

Watching the food go into his mouth, his jaws working like a grinding machine and the gulping swallows, boils up a panic inside me. I run my fingertips along the edges of the cover of my book, pushing on the corners until it hurts.

"You used to say things always look better in the

morning," I say. "Maybe you should just go back to bed."

"This is grown-up stuff, Lia, a little more complicated than that. But it's nothing you have to worry about."

~~Because I am still a little girl who believes in Santa and the tooth fairy and you.~~

He fumbles in the pocket of his robe for his reading glasses. "Is my laptop over there?"

I point to the bookshelf above the television.

"Ah." He stands up and crosses the room. "Why don't you finish this for me?" he says as he shoves the pie (545) in my face.

"I don't want to." I push it back. "It's disgusting."

He frowns. "It won't hurt you. It's just pie."

He keeps the pie plate inches away from my face. If I smacked his hand, the pie would splatter against the entertainment unit and slide down the television screen.

"We don't want your mother to be right about this, do we?" he asks.

"Right about what?" I ask.

"About you slipping back into your old habits. The bad ones."

I stand up, forcing him to step backwards and give me some room. "I'm tired," I say. "I'm going to bed."

My feet on the carpeted stairs do not make a sound. I open the door slowly.

Cassie is gone. The room smells a little like a bakery at Christmas, but she's not here. I set the computer to play country music because she hates it, and crawl into bed.

Just as I start to doze, the music stops.

Cassie sits at the foot of my bed, looking stronger, healthier than before, like she's getting the hang of being a ghost. She pats the shape of my leg under the blankets and says, "Go to sleep. It'll be okay."

There are no spiders in sight, no friendly critters to make her go away. I want to tell her to leave me alone, but my mouth won't open.

◀ 025.00 ▶

Thursday.

I wake up breathing dirt. I cough and spit out the pebbles in my mouth, but when I inhale again, wet clots of clay fill my lungs—

No. It's the sheet trapped over my face. I rip it off and get out of the bed as fast as I can. The house is dark, 5:45. This is the first time in weeks I'm awake before Emma. Down the hall, my father's shower turns on. He probably has another committee meeting.

I turn on all the lights and catch a glimpse of me in the mirror. My metabolism is slowing down again. Yellow bubbles of fat are bloating under my skin. I am starting to look disgusting again, weak.

::Stupid/ugly/stupid/bitch/stupid/fat/
stupid/baby/stupid/loser/stupid/lost::

They gave me rules for moments like this:
1. Identify the feeling.
2. Recite ~~magic incantations~~ affirmations, reread Life Goals, meditate on positive thoughts.
3. Call therapist if negative self-talk continues.
4. Maintain required caloric intake and hydration.
5. Avoid excessive exercise, and alcohol or drug abuse.
6. Click heels together three times, and repeat, "There's no place like home, there's no place like home, there's no place like home." A tornado will be along momentarily to whisk you away to safety. Or a house might drop on your head.

~~Nothing works nothing ever works it just keeps killing me from the inside~~ I lay on the floor for a couple hundred crunches, until sweat pools in my belly button.

New rules:
1. 800 calories a day, max. 500 preferred.
2. A day starts at dinner. If they make me eat with them, stuff in enough to keep them off my back. Restrict during the next day to make up for it.
3. If no breakfast, take the bus to school.

3a. Better—walk.

3b. Best—don't go.

4. Restart exercise program.

5. Sleep with the lights on until they bury her.

I smile and play pretend through the Morning Show in the kitchen. Jennifer is grilling Emma with division flash cards because she has a math test. They barely notice I'm in the room. They are ten minutes late getting out the door.

The Physics teacher demonstrates momentum and collision with a bowling ball and a squash ball. The bowling ball wins. Instead of History we march down to the gym for a college fair. Representatives from a couple hundred schools and the military stand behind card tables loaded with glossy brochures that all promise us a bright and shiny future.

Five thousand acres of trees were slaughtered to make those brochures. They'll all be in the trash by the end of the day. Do I need to pick one up? No. We know where I'm going to college. Do I want to go? No.

What do I want?

The answer to that question does not exist.

I should have kept Cassie's see-glass, or at least looked through it before I gave it back. It would have been better than a dumb brochure.

❊ ❊ ❊

The stage crew invites me to sit at their lunch table. I just want to nap in the nurse's office, but they're being sweet so I say "Sure" and follow them into the lunch line.

I buy a small, bruised apple (70), and a low-fat, artificially sweetened yogurt (60). The girl in front of me, Sasha, buys breaded cheese fingers deep-fried in lard served with tomato sauce. And a brownie. And a bottle of water. The guy in front of her (he runs the light board and the sound) buys spaghetti and pays extra for a second serving of garlic bread. Another guy buys pizza. The girl behind me gets a bowl of lettuce and celery and a small bowl of ketchup. The rest of the girls buy taco salads.

We sit in the middle of the cafeteria, a fish bowl crowded with minnows, guppies, tetras, mollies, and angelfish. Sharks circle their prey. Lesser spiny eels bump their noses against the glass, looking for the exit. Bits of fish flakes and strings of poop dangle in the air. Lime-green algae slicks the floor.

The crew talks about who cried at the wake and who didn't cry and who was crying because they got dumped, not because Cassie's body was laid out in the padded box. When they ask me questions I recite the lines written for me in advance. Yes, it was so tragic. No, I had no idea. Yes, I think the undertaker did a crappy job. No, I don't think she would have liked that dress. Yeah, it was weird. . . .

Their mouths open, close, open-close, gills flaring out and flapping behind their ears. Cheesefinger grease floats to the surface of the water. The janitors will clean it up with sawdust. The pizzafish guy drops sauce on his shirt. A tacosalad girl has an infected nose piercing. She was in my ballet class in seventh grade. Lettuce&ketchup keeps giving me dirty looks, because no matter what she does, she can't lose those last ten pounds.

I cut the mushy bruise out of my apple, slice what's left into eight pieces, dip one into the yogurt and lay it on my tongue, swimmy yummy and soft. It bumps its way down my throat and splashes.

"I've never been to a funeral before," says the blonde tacosalad.

"I've been to tons," says the spaghetti. "My dad's side of the family keeps dying. The funerals are all the same."

"Do we have to shovel the dirt in?" asks the tacosalad with the nose piercing.

"The cemetery does that." Spaghetti crunches into his garlic bread. "They use a small pay loader, like at a construction site."

"We should all go together." Sasha cheesefingers sips her water. "Just like at the wake. It'll mean a lot to her parents."

Cassie swims through the double doors, shoeless, the blue dress rippling against her body. Her hair streams behind her, tangled and braided with seaweed ribbons. Tiny snails are suckered onto her neck and fingers.

She drifts over the first table, scanning the room. I stare deep into my yogurt.

"Do you want to meet us at my house, Lia?" asks the blonde tacosalad. She has salsa on her shirt but she doesn't see it. "I can get my mom's van, we'll all fit."

Cassie swims faster, circling around the bowl, looking for me. I wonder if the see-glass is still in her belly. She'll have to puke it up if she wants to see her future. But maybe that works different when you're dead.

"Lia?"

"I don't think I'm going," I say as Cassie disappears into the kitchen.

"What?"

"My parents don't want me to."

"You have to go," whines lettuce&ketchup. "We all have to go, to show our support."

"What support?" I ask.

"Support for Cassie," she snaps back. "Not that you would know what that is."

"Hey"— I point the plastic knife at her—"I was her friend a lot longer than you were."

"Oh, really?" She pulls her face into the mask of outrage: eyes wide, head jutted forward, mouth hanging open in pretend shock. "Is that why she never talked to you? I know how you messed her up. A real friend would never do that. I'd never do that."

The tables around us listen in. Stage crew is supposed to be mellow and depressed. They never fight in public.

I should just swim away, but my gills flap and angry bubbles come out of my mouth. "If you were her friend, where were you when she was scared and alone?" I ask. "Did you pick up the phone? No. You didn't. You suck."

"What are you talking about? She didn't call me."

Sasha puts her hand on my arm. "Calm down, Lia."

"Calm? How can I be calm? She's dead!"

I am standing. I am screaming. I think I threw my yogurt at lettuce&ketchup.

A fat security guard fish swims over to protect the peace.

◀ 026.00 ▶

As I walk in (stayed late for detention, thank you, no sir, it won't happen again, yes, this is hard on all of us), Jennifer heads out.

"Your father promised to do the grocery shopping today," she says as I hang up my jacket in the front hall closet.

"Let me guess: he's still at the library and he's not answering his phone."

"He left it on the dresser. This damn book is killing

him." She looks like she wants to say more but doesn't. "I'm on my way to the store."

"You need me to do anything?"

"Would you mind vacuuming? The cleaning lady didn't show up again and the rugs are filthy."

The police officer arrives while I'm chasing Emma around the living room with the vacuum cleaner, pretending it's a dragon. I hand over the deadly creature to her and answer the door.

The cop introduces herself, "Detective Margaret Greenfield," and asks if she can come in.

I didn't kill Cassie.

Somehow we wind up in the kitchen, the cop in Dad's chair, me in mine, and Emma on my lap, crushing me.

Ididn'tkillherIdidn'tkillher.

"Just a few questions," the detective says. "Nothing to worry about, we're just tying up the loose ends." She flips open a notebook with a huge yawn. "Sorry about that. Shift change always messes up my sleep. The phone records indicate that she called your phone the night she died."

I answer in a trance. "No, I had no idea that Cassie had called me Saturday night. ~~My phone is in my room~~ I haven't seen my phone since Friday afternoon. Third one I've lost in two years. My dad will be furious."

"He really yelled the last time," Emma adds. She shifts her weight on my lap, driving my hip bones into the wooden seat. "Lia's really going to be in trouble now. He's going to ground her for a hundred years."

"If we can get back to Miss Parrish," the detective says.

I put my finger on Emma's lips. "Shh."

"No, I don't know why Cassie would call me. I hadn't talked to her for months. We weren't friends anymore. No particular reason, just one of those things that happens when you're a senior."

The cop nods as she closes her notebook. "I remember those days," she says. "Thank God they're over."

"Can you tell me what happened to her?" I ask.

"No, I'm sorry. If you think of anything, here's my number." She hands me a card. "Tell your parents to call me if they want. Like I said, this is nothing to worry about. We just want to close the book on this one."

After Emma makes a big stinking deal to Dad and Jennifer about the police visit . . . after I spend a hour calming them down, answering the same questions over and over and over again . . . after Dad calls the detective because he doesn't believe me . . . after Jennifer burns the steak, sets off the smoke alarm, and orders Chinese food . . . after I read Emma a chapter of *Harry Potter* . . . after Jennifer claims the tub for a bubble bath . . . after Dad falls asleep grading papers comparing the election of 1789 to the election of 1792 . . . the house sleeps.

❋ ❋ ❋

The cell phone crawls out of its hiding place under my laundry and sneaks into my hand. As I play her messages over and over, I turn on my computer and visit a country I haven't been to in months, a whispersecretblog for girls like me. . . .

❀ ❀ ❀

Gained .5 lbs between breakfast and after school.
Only water for the rest of the day, and then ill begin fasting again tomorrow. Love you all, girls!

❀ ❀ ❀

❀ ❀ ❀

I blacked out and fell down a flight of stairs so
I ate two bowls of cereal and now I feel so gross.
How long do I have to run to get rid of it?

❀ ❀ ❀

❀ ❀ ❀

Wow, I am such a FAT ASS.
You know its true.
I want to cut it all off.

❀ ❀ ❀

❀ ❀ ❀

I have 2 weeks and 6 days to loose 10 pounds. Help!

❀ ❀ ❀

❀ ❀ ❀

staystrongloveloveBperfekt

❀ ❀ ❀

Hundreds and hundreds and hundreds and hundreds of strange little girls screaming through their fingers. My patient sisters, always waiting for me. I scroll through our confessions and rants and prayers, desperation eating us one slow bloody bite at a time.

Two flies crash into my lampshade, *buzzbuzz*, random leftovers from summer with a few hours left to live. I turn off the lights and they swarm to the computer screen, dancing across uploads of sknnygrrl ribs and hips and collarbones, bones pulled out of their skin and laid on top so they can dry in the sun. Beautiful when seen through the paper wings of out-of-season flies.

I turn off everything and crawl into bed.

The flies throw themselves against the window with wet, angry noises, then hover above me, waiting to crawl into my mouth. Maybe they're Cassie's familiars, escorts from the grave heralding her arrival.

I can't face her alone.

I sneak down the stairs and put Emma's boots on the tread second from the bottom. If Dad comes down for a midnight snack or to work, he'll knock them over and give me a warning.

I head for the basement, lock the door behind me, and put in a couple of sweaty hours on the stair-stepper.

◀ 027.00 ▶

The loudspeaker yanks me out of Friday's English in the middle of a practice test and sends me to Ms. Rostoff's office. She tells me that my stepmother called and I have to leave school early for an emergency shrink appointment.

"Why?" I ask.

"Cassie," Ms. Rostoff says. "Talking about it will help."

My purse slips off my shoulder. It's been doing that all day. "Talking makes things worse."

She glances at her screen. "You'll miss Physics."

"Oh," I say, hiking up the purse strap, "that changes everything."

Dr. Nancy Parker smells like cherry cough drops. I sit on her fat leather couch, purse on the floor, and pull the hideous raspberry-colored afghan over me. She unwraps another Halls. I think she's ~~addicted to~~ suffering from a chemical dependency on the red dye. She should explore that issue.

She turns on the white-noise fan and pops the drop in her mouth. "Your parents are concerned that Cassie's death is triggering you."

The couch faces a floor-to-ceiling wall of books. ~~They are filled with crap.~~ None of them is worth reading. There are no fairy tales, no faerie tails, no sword-swinging princesses or lightning-throwing gods. The pages of sentences of words of letters might as well be mathematical equations marching to their logical conclusions. Cough Drop Nancy is not a doctor. She's an accountant.

"I wonder if there might be two struggles going on." She kicks off her shoes and sits cross-legged. The wrinkles on her face say she's pushing sixty, but yoga classes keep her body as flexible as a girl's. "Confusion and grief about the loss of a friend, and the desire to keep your parents at a distance."

She waits for me to fill the air with words. I don't.

"Or I could be totally wrong," she says, "and none of this is affecting you in the slightest."

Rain pours down the windows.

. . . I started coming here after the first ~~prison~~ *clinic stay* because Dr. N. Parker is a ~~scam artist~~ specialist in ~~crazy teenagers~~ troubled adolescents. I opened my mouth during the first couple of visits and gave her a key to open my head. Ginormous mistake. She brought her lantern and a hard hat and lots of rope to wander through my caves. She laid land mines in my skull that detonated weeks later.

I told her I was pissed because she was moving things around in my brain without permission. She booby-trapped me so that every time I had a simple thought—like, *Physics is a waste of time,* or *I need to charge my phone,* or *Japanese can't be that hard to learn*—the annoying-question-from-hell popped up—*Why do you think that, Lia?*

I couldn't ask myself a question—*Why am I so tired?*—without getting slammed by three or four shrink-supplied answers—*Because my glycogen levels are low,* or *Because I am experiencing an ill-defined sense of loss,* or *Because I've lost touch with reality,* or the ever-popular—*Because I am a whacked-out nut job.*

Once I got angry and mouthed off. I told her she was a pathetic loser and I bet she didn't have any kids or grand-kids or if she did they never called and her husband left her, or maybe it was a girlfriend, you never can tell, and even her own mother gave up on her because she wouldn't live in the real world with breathing people, she stayed sealed in this room with the fake books and the fan blow-ing and rain on the windows.

Nothing I said made her angry. I couldn't even make her blink. She just asked me to stay in the feeling and keep talking. So I shut up.

I used to dream about bringing a knife to therapy and *slicing her into pork chop–sized pieces.*

Ten minutes have gone by. As the couch warms up, I sink deeper into the cushions. The leather creaks.

"What words are in your head right now, Lia?"

Pissed. Pig. Hate.

"I'd like to hear them."

Jail. Coffin. Cut.

"You have to work at recovery, Lia. Suspended animation isn't much of a life."

"My weight is fine. I can bring in Jennifer's stupid notebook if you want."

"It's not about the number on the scale. It never was."

Hungry. Dead.

Twenty minutes spin by. I weave my fingers in and out of the afghan. She is Charlotte, I am Wilbur

::Some Girl!/Useless!/Delirious!::

and this pink crocheted nightmare (polyester yarn) is her web. No, she's not Charlotte, she's Charlotte's annoying cousin Mildred, the stupid one, whose webs always break. If my parents had let me invest the money they wasted on this lady, I'd have my own apartment by now.

Forty minutes. I have plucked stray hairs from at least seven different people out of the afghan: a long black one, a shiny white one, a wispy blonde, a curly auburn, a brown hair that was white at the root, and a short hair that could have been a guy's—or a girl's who doesn't fuss with the way she looks. The hair of rich people who like to whine to strangers.

"You didn't have to come here today," she finally says. "You could have used the excuse of a therapy appointment to get out of class and do whatever you wanted. I don't report back to your parents unless you give me permission, so they wouldn't know it if you didn't show up."

"What's your point?" I ask.

"You chose to come." She cracks the knuckles on her right hand and wiggles her fingers. "I think you want to talk about some of this."

~~Yes, I'd love to tell you that Cassie's voice is on the phone in my purse and she is haunting me because I let her die. If I do, you'll give me even more drugs. If I tell you what I ate today, you'll pull the alarm and send me back to jail.~~ I lay all the hairs on the arm of the chair. "I keep thinking that if I could just unzip my skin, step out of this body, then I would see who I really am."

She nods her head slowly. "What do you think you'd look like?"

"Smaller, for a start."

The final eight minutes march past in silent formation until the timer on her desk dings.

"So, can I go to the funeral?" I ask.

She reaches for her shoes. "Do you understand why you want to go to the funeral?"

~~To make sure they bury her in concrete so she'll leave me alone.~~ "I feel that I need some closure about this."

"And the funeral will provide that?"

~~Yes, that's what I just said.~~ "I've given it a lot of thought."

The clock ticks by two bonus minutes. I roll the hair of the strangers into a ball.

"It's a good idea." She slips her shoes on and stands up. "But have one of your parents go with you. Nobody should ever go to a funeral alone."

On the way home, I take the phone out of my purse and the memory out of my phone and lay it on the iron rail just beyond the railroad crossing near the mall. I place the phone itself under the left rear tire and drive back and forth over it thirty-three times. I pitch the remains in a construction site Dumpster.

◀ 028.00 ▶

Elijah opens the door to room 115 with the security chain still latched and presses his face into the small space. His eyes are sleep-swollen and confused.

"Emma?" he asks. "What's up?"

I don't know how to explain the name thing yet. "I brought you pizza. Free food."

The chain rattles and the door opens all the way. "What's the catch?"

The warm mozzarella grease has soaked through the bottom of the box and is leaking into my fingers. ~~I want to lick~~ I want to throw the box away before it infects me.

"No catch."

He leans against the door frame. "There's always a catch."

"It's for helping me out the other night."

"What kind of pizza is it?"

"Extra cheese and sausage."

He smiles. "I can't eat it. I'm a vegetarian."

"I don't believe you."

A door opens at the far end of the motel and a man shouts in a language I can't understand. The woman he's yelling at laughs like a cartoon jackal. Tires screech on River Road and an engine races.

He rubs his face once and steps back. "Okay, I'm mostly a vegetarian. I'm a pizzatarian. Come on in."

The room smells like cigarettes and clothes left in the washing machine too long. The only light comes from a small lamp on the table, squeezed between a stack of spiral notebooks topped with a dirty ashtray and a six-pack of beer.

He takes the pizza box from me and puts it on the bed. Playing cards are scattered over the tangled blankets and thin pillows are piled against the headboard. "What time is it?" he asks.

"Almost five."

"Damn. I must have fallen asleep. Charlie wanted me to fix the shelves in 204. Oh, well. He needs to accept what the universe gives him."

"That's a lame excuse for ditching work."

"No, it's not. Things happen for a reason." He yawns

and stretches. "You gotta accept that and let the flow carry you, stop resisting."

"That's crap."

His eyes are brighter now, mischievous. "One guy's crap is another guy's fertilizer." He waves at the walls. "Ask them."

The walls are covered floor to ceiling with pages torn from books, some highlighted with red or yellow or green markers. I lean forward and squint through the gloom to read. The top of the page says WALDEN.

"What did you do—rob a library?"

"Something like that," he says, walking toward the bathroom. "Emerson, Thoreau, Watts. Sonya Sanchez, ever read her? The Bible, a couple pages. The Bhagavad Gita. Dr. Seuss, Santayana. I put them up to create a force field of good ideas. They soak into my brain while I'm sleeping. Hang on, I got to take care of business." He closes the door.

I pick up the notebook on top of the pile on the table and flip through it. He's pasted random newspaper articles in here and drawn faces; he's not half bad. Charlie at the front desk. A tired woman with her hair in curlers. There are more creatures, half human, half something else, like the thing on his arm. Some pages are filled with tiny hand-writing that looks like ants marching across the page.

Elijah comes out of the bathroom holding a roll of toilet paper. "You know, the secrets of the universe are written in there. You should feel real special, being allowed to snoop like that."

"Sorry." I set it back on the pile. "You're not from around here, are you?"

He tosses the toilet paper roll on the pillows, flips opens the box, and takes out a slice of pizza. "New Jersey." He takes a bite and the cheese strings like a suspension bridge from his mouth to his hand. "Want some?"

~~One bite, please, and then another and another, crust and cheese sausage sauce another and another~~ empty is strong and invincible. "I already ate."

"All the more for me." He sits on the bed. "Want to play poker?"

"No, thanks."

He scoops up a handful of cards: diamonds and spades. "What's your poison: Texas hold 'em or five-card draw? How much cash do you have?"

"I said no. You just want to take my money."

He folds the pizza in half and takes another bite. "Damn right," he says through the mess in his mouth. "But you'll learn a lot while I'm doing it. I'm one of the best cheats around."

I put my left hand behind my back and dig my fingernails into my palm until the pain takes away that ~~lovely~~ wicked smell. "I don't know how to play."

"I'm appalled. How old are you?"

"Eighteen."

"You can vote and join the army, but you can't play poker? Someone has neglected your education, young Emma." He shuffles the cards like a pro. "Have a seat. I'll teach you."

I take two steps toward the door, shaking my head back and forth and fighting a smile. "Sorry. The universe is telling me it's time to go home. See? I'm going with the flow, flowing out to the parking lot."

"Got it. That's cool." Elijah uses toilet paper to wipe tomato sauce off the face of the jack of diamonds. "Wait. I have a question. You know where I can find a good junk-yard? Charlie claims there isn't one in the whole state. That El Camino out there is mine, but it's not going anywhere without a new distributor."

"You get parts for your car from a junkyard?" I ask.

"Don't you? It's the cheapest way to go, plus it's recycling."

"My dad might know." I zip up my jacket. "I'll ask him. He's good with cars."

"Cool. Thanks." He points to the box. "You sure you don't want a piece for the road?"

~~Yes, of course, I do.~~ "No, thanks."

I stand there. And stand there.

Waiting.

"I thought you were going." Elijah pops a piece of sausage in his mouth. "Need a good-bye kiss? I'm happy to oblige."

"No." I drive my fingernails into my palm again for

motivation. "Look," I say. "I have a confession to make. That is not just a thank-you pizza."

"I knew it!" He pumps a fist in the air. "You've fallen in love with me. You want to have my babies. We'll get a team of horses and a covered wagon and we'll journey to South America and raise goats."

"Only in your dreams." I clear my throat. "I brought the pizza to bribe you."

"I can be bribed."

Deep breath. "I need you to go to Cassie's funeral with me. Saturday morning."

He grins again. "See? You're asking me out."

"No, I'm not, you idiot. It's a funeral. A horrible funeral and I don't know who else to ask."

He tears off a piece of crust. "What's in it for me?"

"I just gave you a pizza."

"Not enough. Funerals bring out the worst in people. They have a very dark vibe." He shakes his head. "Nope, I can't do it."

"You have to."

"No, I don't."

I chew the inside of my cheek. "How about a game of cards? If I win, you go with me."

"What if you lose?"

I swallow. "If I lose, I'll give you fifty dollars. But only on one condition."

"See? I told you. There's always a catch. What is it?"

"We play hearts, not poker."

◀ 029.00 ▶

When I get home, Jennifer and Dad are snuggled on the couch in front of the gas-fed fireplace, flames on low, chick flick playing on the big screen. Jennifer is massaging lotion into Dad's right wrist and hand. All the extra typing on his overdue book must have aggravated his carpal tunnel.

"Where's Emma?" I ask. "She's not in bed already, is she?"

"She's sleeping over at the Grants'," Jennifer says. "Against my better judgment."

"Why?" I ask.

Jennifer pours more lotion into her palm. "Her last soccer tournament is tomorrow, all day. She's going to be exhausted. I still think we should have kept her home."

"Let the child have some fun." Dad winces a little as Jennifer kneads his wrist. "In ten years, no one will remember how she played in this tournament." He looks up at me. "Were you at the library again?"

"A friend's house. Mira's," I lie. "We studied a little physics, but mostly we played cards and ate pizza."

"That's wonderful," Dad says, beaming. "You haven't done that in ages."

Jennifer keeps her eyes on her work, the pads of her thumbs rubbing circles into the heel of his hand. "How was your meeting with Dr. Parker?" she asks.

~~None of your freaking business.~~ "Good. I'm glad I went. We talked about Cassie."

"Excellent," Dad says. "I'm very proud of you."

"Thanks. I'm going to bed. I'm beat."

"Hang on." Jennifer sets his hand in his lap and finally looks at me. "What about the funeral?"

I pause in the doorway that leads to the hall. "She said it was a good idea. I'm going with Mira and a bunch of girls from the drama club."

"If you feel uncomfortable," Jennifer says, "don't hesitate to leave. If you change your mind and want one of us to go with you, it's not a problem."

"I'll be okay."

As I turn to leave, Jennifer adds, "Wait, one more thing."

I turn back around.

"I talked to your mother again today," Jennifer says, ignoring the look of surprise on Dad's face.

"Yeah?" I have a bad feeling about this.

"I promised her I'd try to convince you to spend the night at her house tomorrow."

I knew it.

"I don't want to," I say. "I don't see any point."

"I know," Jennifer says. "You're an adult, you make your own decisions. We're beginning to figure that out." She smiles a little and it softens her words. "Sometimes being an adult means doing the right thing, even if it's not what you want."

"I don't see how it's the right thing," I say. "Mom and me can't talk without screaming. It's better if we're not around each other."

"You haven't spent time with her in months," Jennifer points out. "Maybe that's changed."

Dad's head goes back and forth, like he's watching a tennis game but doesn't understand the language being spoken by the announcers.

"Just one night," Jennifer says. "Think of what a good example you'd show Emma—how to deal head-on with things that make you uncomfortable. Everybody has to learn how to do that."

It's cheating to bring up Emma like that. Advantage: Jennifer.

"Fine," I say. "One night. But you tell her. I hate talking to her on the phone."

I take a long shower and wash my pushy stepmother and my confused father and the smell of cheese, sausage, and motel out of my hair.

I did win one thing today. I shot the moon in hearts and beat Elijah. I'm picking him up at ten tomorrow. Neither one of us is up to the memorial service at the funeral home. We're going straight to the grave. The drive will give me the chance to explain the confusion about my name, if he shuts his mouth for more than thirty seconds.

Maybe we'll run away to South America after the funeral and raise goats.

※ ※ ※

Cassie grows braver every night, coming sooner, staying longer, freaking me out more and more. Once her coffin is tucked into the ground and the magic prayers are said and flowers are laid on top of her, she'll go to sleep forever.

But I need to get some sleep. I pop a sleeping pill and tiptoe down the stairs in my robe for a mug of chamomile tea.

The movie has finished and Jennifer and Dad are talking quietly, the Weather Channel droning in the background. I pause at the corner of the kitchen, listening for kissing sounds. I hate walking in on them when they're making out.

I peek around the corner. No kissing. Just talking, each of them occupying a corner of the couch with pillows in between.

Husband: You're overreacting. She's a little stressed, but she's trying.

Wife: She doesn't look good.

Husband: You see the scales every week.

Wife: I wish she'd go in for a checkup. Have some blood work.

Husband: We can only suggest it. To be honest, pushing the issue might make things worse.

Wife: Chloe wants her to move back in.

Husband, picking up remote and adjusting flames of fireplace: Not just visit for a night?

Wife: She's afraid Lia is out of control again. I agree. A couple months with her mom might help get her back on track.

Husband: You were the one who convinced me to let her move in. You can't change your mind just because she's hit a rough patch. What are you going to do when Emma goes through this? Send her to Chloe's house, too?

Wife: Don't be ridiculous. Emma and Lia are very different people.

Husband: She had pizza with friends tonight. She's fine. You and Chloe are blowing this out of proportion. Now, what time do we have to get up in the morning?

Cassie is waiting for me upstairs. She heard everything.

I try to ignore her, but every time I turn around, she materializes in front of my eyes. We slide into the computer and scroll through the chorus.

❀ ❀ ❀

im bulimic have been for six years recently tried to recover gained a lot of weight now im slipping back and cant stand the weight any longer

❀ ❀ ❀

❀ ❀ ❀

what does everyone think is the least amount of days you could lose 25 pounds?

❀ ❀ ❀

❀ ❀ ❀

i try to keep calorie intake under 500.

anything more is unacceptable.

Mucho Love! stay strong <333

❀ ❀ ❀

❀ ❀ ❀

i am so disgustingly, horribly fat. Today i went for a 2

hour run and starved myself till dinner where i ate

like a pig. Sometimes i feel so fucking helpless.

❀ ❀ ❀

❀ ❀ ❀

i am on a HIGH here. i think i might finally be

getting pretty good at this! to those of you

who are having a tough time right now, big hugs.

you can do anything if you try hard enough!

❀ ❀ ❀

When the house is asleep, I turn off the music and light a candle. Cassie sits on the windowsill and watches as I draw three razor lines, perfectly straight, on my right hip.

Now it matches the left.

◀ 030.00 ▶

On my way to pick up Elijah Saturday morning, I stop at a store to buy a map and a compass. The GPS is on my Christmas list, in ink. What I really need is a crystal ball, but nobody sells them around here.

I open up the compass box as soon as I'm in the car. The compass is defective. No matter how I hold it, the little needle spins and spins around the dial without stopping.

I want my money back.

Elijah spends more time talking about his plans to drive south after Christmas than navigating. We get lost right after leaving the motel and waste time driving on roads that aren't on the map. When we finally pull in between the stone griffins at the entrance to Mountain View Cemetery, we're late.

A thin man in a long black coat and a black cowboy hat points me to a small parking lot. My car is the third one there.

I get out, wishing I had worn sweatpants, because the air smells like snow. I tug at the hem of my dress and shiver. This girl looked almost pretty in the mirror this morning: clean hair, decent makeup, antique silver earrings, a spider-gray short-sleeved dress (size zero) that fluttered just above her knees, and killer high heels. I forgot about it being thirty-seven degrees out.

"You sure we're in the right place?" Elijah asks as we close the doors.

The man with the hat walks over to us. "If you folks hustle, you might make it up there before the graveside service begins."

"Up where?" I ask.

"Up that hill," he says, pointing to a steep road. "The Parrish service is at the top. You'll have to walk. All the parking spaces up there are filled. Good day." He gives the tiniest of bows and walks back to his position at the gate.

"I'll never make it in these," I say, pointing to my shoes. "I can barely walk to the bathroom in them."

"So why'd you wear them?" Elijah asks. He's wearing dark jeans, work boots, the shirt and tie he wore to the wake, and a camouflage jacket. His earring is a solid black plug.

"They look good."

"No, they don't," he says. "If they hurt you, they're hideous." He hunches over slightly and bends his knees. "Come on," he says. "Jump on my back."

"What?"

"I'll carry you up there. I mean, it'll probably kill me, but I'll go out in a blaze of glory."

"That's not necessary." I open the trunk of my car and

root around until I find a pair of old high-top sneakers, dingy white and covered in blue-ink flowers drawn during History class. "I'll wear these."

I sit on the bumper, take off the heels, and put on the sneakers, which smell like they've been cooking in a trunk full of garbage for a year or so, but they make my toes happy.

I stand up. "Sophisticated, huh?"

Elijah takes in the sneakers, the dress, and the fact that I'm shivering. He takes off his jacket and gives it to me. "Don't even think about arguing."

His jacket is heavy with the heat from his body and smells like gasoline and boy. "Thanks."

"Now," he says, eyeing me up and down a second time. "Now you look good."

◀ 031.00 ▶

I don't feel good by the time we make it to the top. The fresh cuts in my hip are aching and I'm certain one of them has opened up and is bleeding. Every step closer to Cassie makes me colder and weaker. It's affecting Elijah, too. He walks with his head down and hands shoved in his pockets.

The crest of the hill is covered with hundreds of black-backed beetles gathered for the carrion feast: kids from school, teachers, the parents who show up at everything.

The members of the stage crew are grouped in threes and fours. The soccer team is one solid block, most wearing their team jackets. I don't see my mother anywhere.

"How close do you want to be?" Elijah quietly asks me.

"As close as we can get."

He sighs. "Okay. Follow me."

We make our way through the crowd toward the white pavilion tent. Cassie's parents and other relatives sit inside on plastic chairs, listening to the minister, who stands with one hand on Mr. Parrish's shoulder.

The coffin is covered with a thick blanket of pale pink roses. It's resting on a metal brace like a hot cookie sheet cooling on a rack. Strips of fake grass are supposed to hide the brace, but the wind has peeled them away.

I stand on my tiptoes. If we were closer, we could see to the bottom of the hole.

Cassie's parents can. The mouth of the grave is inches away from their feet.

A beehive-shaped pile of dirt is mounded behind the tent, waiting for the end of the service. The grave diggers will dump the dirt in the hole to keep Cassie from floating to the surface and running away.

The mountains to the north have disappeared under a snowstorm. Down here the wind screams over the rows of thunder-colored headstones. I close my eyes.

Cassie's pet mouse, Pinky, died the summer before fourth grade. She cried so hard I thought we were going to have to call an ambulance, or at least my mom. I helped her downstairs. Her mother was off somewhere, and her dad was in charge, watching the Red Sox play the Yankees. He told Cassie to stop crying. He'd put the corpse in the trash after the game.

Cassie held it together until we got back to her room, then she threw herself on her bed and wailed, "I don't want to put him in the trash."

"We won't," I said. "We'll give him a proper funeral."

I used a spatula to lift Pinky out of his cage and lay him on Cassie's favorite blue bandanna. I rolled him up like a mousy burrito and tied it with yarn. I told Cassie she should carry him, but when she touched the bandanna she shrieked. I put on oven mitts and carried Pinky to the side yard. Cassie followed with a little shovel.

The easiest place to dig was in the middle of her mom's rose garden. We took turns scraping away the new mulch and digging a hole between two bushes, one marked *Mordent Blush*, the other *Nearly Wild*, each sign handwritten with a calligraphy pen.

I faked a little Latin and chanted most of the Lord's Prayer. Cassie added long "ooooommmms" that she claimed was Chinese. (Her parents encouraged her to explore other cultures.) While she omed, I laid Pinky in the hole and covered him with dirt.

"Sure hope a dog doesn't dig him up," I said.

Her face crumpled.

"Hang on."

I ran across the street and grabbed a plastic bucket of beach stones from my room. We laid the stones on the grave, spread mulch on top, and chanted a couple more prayers. We stood, holding hands, eyes closed, and swore that we would never, ever forget our special Pinky.

The summer after that one, her mom's Nearly Wild won the Greater Manchester Rose Grower Association's grand prize. The newspaper did a full-color spread on the garden and *the Parrishes threw a party to celebrate.*

The preacher stands at the head of the coffin and puts out his arms to call down the gods. He thanks everyone for coming, and then his voice drops and it's impossible to hear him. A few more late stragglers rush up the hill, trying to move quickly without being seen. One of them is a tall woman in boots and a long mink coat, her yellow hair pulled back in a flawless French braid, prescription sunglasses that she doesn't need because the clouds are black and low.

My mother.

I move behind Elijah. "Block the wind for me, okay?"

"What?" he asks. "Sure."

I count to ten, then peek out around his shoulder. She's standing at the edge of the crowd, just past the soccer team, nodding and half smiling at the people around her.

Some guy walks up to the preacher and whispers in his ear, maybe explaining that no one can hear a word the guys says because of the wind blowing.

The preacher nods and shouts, "Let us pray!"

I lean my forehead against Elijah's sturdy back.

The day we buried Nanna Marrigan, I walked behind my mother through the cemetery, her hand shooting out from time to time to warn me about tripping on exposed roots. I was thirteen. We passed under dying oaks, sharp-eyed crows pacing on their branches, and by teenage angels frozen in marble, cobwebs strung from their heads to their thin shoulders.

Nanna was waiting in her coffin, next to the fresh hole dug at the back of the cemetery, where they planted the new dead. She had picked out the coffin and the hymns and the prayers. She demanded that people contribute to the library instead of sending flowers.

The minister gave us little booklets so we could follow along, but I didn't take one. My mother cried without crumpling up her face because Nanna didn't like it when people made a spectacle of themselves in public. I was so stunned by the sight of the tears streaming down her cheeks I missed most of the service.

The grave diggers lifted my grandmother's coffin as if it were filled with feathers. As they lowered it into the ground, the wind blew and ghostshadows unfolded and folded themselves like butterflies on the ground. The marble girls whispered and the ghostshadows *snuck inside and hid behind my ribs.* . . .

※ ※ ※

I open my eyes. The minister is still quoting his Bible. Elijah's face is tilted up to the sky, perfectly calm. Mira from school is sobbing, her father's arm around her shoulders. My mother has her head bowed, her lips moving. I wish I knew what she prays for.

Mrs. Parrish leans against her husband. He lays his cheek on the top of her head, his arms and hands holding her tight so she doesn't jump in. The rose petals on the coffin flutter in the wind. A few are ripped off and sucked straight up into the sky.

The rest of the mourners shiver as the storm slides down from the north. Restless clouds of ghosts swirl paths from grave to sticky grave.

"Amen!" the minister shouts into the wind.

◀ 032.00 ▶

Game over.

The man in black hollers that we're all invited back to the family's home to continue the celebration of Cassie's life and find strength in one another. As Cassie's parents walk away from the tent, my mother approaches them and says something. They take turns hugging her, Mom patting them gently on the back.

"Funerals suck," Elijah says to me. "Next time we bet, we're playing poker. Ready to go?"

"Not quite," I say. "I want to watch them cover her up."

He chews the inside of his cheek. "I'll wait for you at

the car. The dead people are weirding me out."

"Lia!" The wind almost blows her voice away, but not quite.

Damn. She saw me.

I step behind Elijah. "Don't move." He tries to turn around but I poke him in the ribs. "I mean it."

"What's going on?" he asks. "Who are you hiding from?"

"My mother."

He starts to turn around again. "Why?"

I grab his shirt to keep him from moving. "Just don't let her see me."

I huddle against his back, my face behind the curtain of my hair. Car doors are opening and shutting, engines turning over, tires crunching on the gravel.

"Why not?" he asks.

. . . The second time they admitted me,

. . . the second time they locked me up, I was bad, bad, bad. My parental units were frowny mad, mad, mad. Dead, rotting daughters leave a bad smell that won't come out no matter how hard the cleaning lady scrubs. My parents bounced the blame back and forth, bouncing Lia bean, sick starving Lia bean, what is wrong with her, it's all your faultfaultfault.

My mother wanted to be the boss, wanted to be Dr. Marrigan instead of Sick Lia's Mom. That didn't work. The clinic docs dug a moat around me and said she could not swim across it, she had to wait until she was invited to cross the drawbridge. After that, she missed a couple of family therapy sessions. She tried to explain why, but my ears were stuffed with bread and pasta and milk shakes.

I limped alongside the other rag-doll girls. One had a plastic door cut in her belly so she could dump the food in without using her mouth. When she got angry, she would puke the food out the belly door, slam it shut, and lock herself.

I had to shave my furry legs in front of a nurse so I didn't accidentally open a vein. When I was a pink, hairless mouse, she took away the razor. I curled up in a matchbox filled with sawdust and covered my face with my cold rope tail. The shrinks dug into their bag of tricks and doled out new pills, my crazy candies, baby blue and nap-time gray.

They experimented on me for weeks. 089.00. 090.60. 093.00. 095.00. They stuffed the Lia-piñata with melted cheese and bread crumbs. 099.00. 103.00. 104.00. 105.00. 106.00. They released me at 108.00 with a three-ring slut-red binder that held all of my lessons: meal plans, follow-up appointments, ~~magic incantations~~ affirmations to keep away the nasty thoughts.

I refused to return to the house of my mother. If I was such a difficult child, such a pain in her neck, then I'd find someplace else to live. She tried to talk me out of it, but I pulled up the drawbridge, locked it with iron bars, and posted an armed guard.

The doctors gave Dad and Jennifer a black slippery

bag filled with jingle-bell bottles *of crazy seeds, perfect mini-castanets*, shooka, shooka, shooka.

Elijah cracks his knuckles. "Why don't you want to see your mom?"

"Do you like your parents?" I ask.

"Love my mom. Dad beat the crap out of me, then kicked me out."

"Oh," I say. "I'm sorry."

"Hang on," he says. "We need to spin left a little." He twists slightly to keep his body between me and the eyes of my mother.

"Thanks," I say. "Is she looking this way?"

"She was, but then two ladies holding umbrellas tackled her. Now they're bashing her in the face with their purses. Why don't you want to see her? Did she burn your dolls in a sacrificial fire? Read your e-mail?"

"She wants to run my life," I explain.

"What a bitch. It's like she thinks she's your mother or something."

"She's a psychopath," I said. "It's complicated."

"Psychopaths can't afford fur coats."

"This one can. What is she doing now?"

"Her head is spinning three hundred and sixty degrees and she's spewing frogs," he says.

"What are you—?" I poke my head out around his shoulder.

She is standing only three graves away. "Lia?" she calls.

"Lia?" Elijah echoes.

He steps to the side and takes away my hiding place.

I step on the closest grave—Fanny Lott, 1881–1924—hoping the earth will collapse under me. It doesn't.

"What are you doing here?" ~~Mom~~ Dr. Marrigan asks.

"Um," I say.

"Your name is Lia?" Elijah asks.

"I thought we agreed you wouldn't come," she says.

"Hold on." Elijah raises his hand for attention. "You're Lia, the friend Cassie was trying to call. Why didn't you answer your phone that night?"

Dr. Marrigan scans him in a nanosecond. "Who is this?"

"This is my friend, Elijah. Elijah, my mother, Dr. Chloe Marrigan."

She steps in between us. "Excuse us. I need to talk to my daughter."

Elijah shivers and tries to hide it. "Why didn't you tell me your real name?"

Along the road, cars are put into low gear for the slow ride down the hill.

"I'm sorry about that," I say. "I can explain."

"You have a lot of explaining to do," Dr. Marrigan says.

"No, I don't, Mother," I snap. "Dr. Parker told me I

could come, not that it's any of your business. Nothing I do is your business anymore."

Elijah winces at the razor blades in my voice.

Dr. Marrigan opens her mouth to say more, but a man and a woman call out her name. I don't recognize them, but she does and turns away from me to talk to them.

"Okay, so she's intense," Elijah says quietly. "Not a psychopath, but a little wired."

"She hates it when I think for myself," I say.

Mom is wearing the friendly face, good for shaking hands after church and running into former patients at the grocery store. She does not introduce me.

"You look like her," Elijah says. "Except for the color of your hair."

"That is not a compliment."

"She really pushes your buttons, doesn't she?" he asks.

"She's gifted that way."

"And you deal with it by running away?"

"It worked for you."

He crosses his arms over his chest. "Not really."

I really should give him back his jacket, but I'll freeze in an instant and she'll say something awful and I'll break into tiny pieces.

Elijah unfolds his arms and blows on his fingers. "Even if your mom is a nut job, she's reaching out to you. You gotta respect that."

"That's not reaching out, that's choking."

The funeral director's assistant is folding up the fake

grass strips under the tent. A man in a red hunting jacket is driving a tiny backhoe to the grave. The wind blows the assistant's hat off his head and he chases it.

As the couple walks away, Dr. Marrigan turns to us again. "I have to go to the hospital to check on a patient. You'll be at the house when I get back, right?"

Elijah nudges my sneaker with his boot.

"Right," I say, without thinking. "But I have to drop off Elijah first."

She blinks rapidly, trying to recover her balance. She was bracing for a fight and didn't get it.

"Okay, then," she says, slightly uncertain. "I'll see you there. Be careful driving."

"Right."

As she walks away, the assistant under the tent picks up a small remote and presses a button, sending Cassie's casket into the ground.

◀ 033.00 ▶

Elijah and I walk back to the car without a word.

"Are you mad at me?" I finally ask as I unlock the car. "About the name thing?"

"I don't think so," he says.

"I can explain—" I start.

He holds up both hands to stop me. "Could we not talk for a while?" he says quietly. "My head's a little crowded.

Dead people and angry parents are not a good combination for me. I need to chill."

"Okay."

We are silent until we arrive at the Gateway. I park in front of his room and hand him his jacket.

"I really appreciate everything you did today."

"No worries. Thanks for the ride." He takes the jacket, gets out of the car, shuts the door, and walks away.

I roll down my window. "Wait. When can we talk again?"

"I don't know." He pulls his keys out of his pocket.

"I forgot to ask my dad about the junkyard," I say. "I'll call you when I find out where it is."

"Thanks." He disappears inside the darkness of his room.

I'm not sure why his mood shifted. Maybe there's something in the air of graveyards, it penetrates the skin and infects. Maybe that's why I suddenly feel sick, too. A wave of nausea bulldozes through my belly: sadmadbadconfused, everything gags me. I fight back the pictures in my head: roses shivering on her coffin, tears falling to the ground, clouds of sorrow racing toward us on the storm. I choke and cough. If I had eaten anything today, it'd be coming up right now.

A red warning light pops up next to my speedometer. I dig around in my purse for my phone so I can call Dad and ask him if the engine is going to explode, but I don't have a phone anymore.

I crank the heat up to FULL and put my nose up to the vent. The air smells like Cassie and makes me choke again.

~~I'm hungry I need to eat.~~

I hate eating.

~~I need to eat.~~

I hate eating.

~~I need to eat.~~

I love not-eating.

The red oil light blinks ON/OFF, ON/OFF, ON/OFF. I shift out of PARK and accelerate.

◀ 034.00 ▶

Briarwood Avenue is lined with made-to-order houses. There are no sidewalks here, no front porches. The lawns are trained to roll quietly from the front door down to the road, each blade of grass hand-trimmed to the regulation height. Usually the street is empty and swept clean.

Not today. Cars are parked along both sides of the road, wheels making muddy impressions on the fringes of the lawns. Metal doors slam, security systems chirp, black-coated people with frowns bend into the wind and shuffle to the house across the street from my mother's.

They're here to pay their dues, pay respects, pay the price of knowing a dead girl's parents. They're going to Cassie's house.

I park in my mother's driveway.

Mrs. Parrish's rose garden has spread out along both sides of the house and taken over the front yard. The bushes are pruned down to thorny spikes for winter, wrapped in burlap sacks, summer dreams of fat blossoms pulled deep into the roots.

The first time I saw Cassie puke was in that garden. Her parents were having a Labor Day party, the last one before school started. The grown-ups were loud and drunk in the pool, the high-school couples had retreated home to the soft couches waiting in empty basements, and the little kids were in bed. We weren't little anymore; we were eleven. We could stay up as long as we wanted if we didn't bug our parents.

I ran across the street to my house to get a sweatshirt. When I came back, Cassie was gone. I hunted everywhere until I found her in the shadows of the rose garden, away from the torchlights and the sound of margarita blenders. She was gagging, finger shoved down her throat. Most everything she had eaten was splashed on the mulch: a bag of potato chips, most of a carton of onion dip, two fudge brownies, and a slice of strawberry shortcake.

"I'll get your mom," I said.

"No!" She grabbed me and explained in tight, cramped

whispers. She was puking on purpose, so she wouldn't get fat. She started to cry because she had waited too long and calories were leaking into her and making her feel bad.

"Why did you eat the brownies, if you don't want to get fat?" my little elf-girl body asked.

"Because I was hungry!" Tears spilled down her cheeks and rolled into the nastiness on her chin.

I kicked mulch on the mess and snuck her up to the bathroom so she could wash her hair. I cleaned the puke off her shirt with the Dove soap in the sink, gagging the whole time. When she was in the shower, I stuck her shirt in the dryer. I used a butter knife to scrape off the nasty smell from the soap.

Buried in our sleeping bags later, she told me that every girl in her cabin at drama camp puked. When I asked why, she said it was because they were all fat-fat-fatties and something had to be done. Camp taught Cassie way more than school.

By eighth grade she had turned pro, color-coding the beginning of her binges either Doritos orange or blueberry purple so she'd know when the job was done. Her favorite puking finger was lined with scratches that never healed. She told her mom they were from soccer/lacrosse practice or play practice/set construction. Or that the dog nipped her.

Cassie became the roller coaster in the theme park of middle school. I was the merry-go-round horse frozen in one position, *eyes painted open, paint chipping off my eyes.* . . .

I should dig up the Nearly Wild and take out Pinky's matchstick bones still warm in the blue bandanna. I should knit them into a sweater or string them on a ribbon and wear it around my neck. If I still had the green see-glass, I would work it in, too. Whenever I was lost, I could hold it up to my eye. Much better than a spinning compass.

The empty-gas-tank warning pops up next to the blinking red light. No problem.

~~My mother~~ Dr. Marrigan pulls into the driveway. She looks at me through the glass in her window and the glass in mine while the garage door opens. Her nose is red and her eyes swollen, like she's been crying. She turns her head away from me and drives into the garage.

I stay in the car for a few minutes, then follow her.

◀ 035.00 ▶

I'm sure she's waiting for me in the family room, temperature at fifty-eight degrees, her lecture notes neatly arranged with my faults and mistakes listed in order of priority. She has charts to prove everything I do is wrong, and that my only hope is to allow them to insert her stem cells in my marrow so she can grow a new her dressed in my skin.

But, no. She's not in the family room.

She's waiting for me in the library, which normal people call the "living room."

Nope. Miles of dusted bookshelves, cardiology journals stacked on the coffee table. No Dr. Marrigan.

Not in the kitchen.

Not on the treadmill in the basement. Not on the elliptical or lifting weights or working her abs.

"Mom?"

The pipes in the basement shudder and the hot-water tank fires up. She must be taking a shower.

I go up two flights and tiptoe across the polished floor of her bedroom, slooooooowly turn the doorknob, and open her bathroom door a crack. A breath of steam trickles out, filled with the sobs of a grown woman breaking into girl-sized pieces.

I close the door.

When she comes downstairs an hour later, coffee is brewing, orange juice is poured, and a place is set for her at the table with Nanna Marrigan's bone china, the antique silver from the giant chest in the dining room, and a linen napkin the color of snow. The way she likes it—precise and neat. Just so.

The tears have been washed away, but her nose is still red. She looks around the kitchen, confused and off balance again, because I am not following the script.

I hand her the glass of juice. As she sips it, I crack

open three eggs and turn on the burner under the frying pan to melt the butter.

Every step in a kitchen is a test—*I am strong enough to pick up a stick of butter. I am strong enough to peel off the paper wrapper, drop a hunk in the pan, and watch-listensmell it melt.* I wash the greasy smear off my fingertips without tasting it. I am passing all the tests today with flying colors.

"When did you learn to cook?" my mother asks.

"Jennifer showed me. Emma loves omelets."

She sniffs the air. "Is there something in the oven?"

"I wanted to make carrot-raisin muffins—Emma likes those, too. But you didn't have carrots or raisins, so those are nutmeg muffins." I beat the eggs. "Your refrigerator is kind of empty. There's only onion or spinach for your omelet."

She studies the chopped veggies on the cutting board. "Just spinach."

I pour her coffee into the china cup and give it to her. She sets it on the table, then pulls her phone and beeper out of her robe pocket and lines them up next to the fork. She drifts into the chair, eyes unfocused on her reflection in the empty plate.

"Who was it?" I ask.

She looks up. "Who was who?"

I slowly pour the eggs into the hot pan. "Which patient died?"

"How do you know a patient died?"

I lift the skin of the omelet to let wet egg slide underneath it. "The only time you cry in the shower like that is when you lose a patient."

The pan sizzles. The oven timer dings.

Mom spreads the napkin in her lap. "She was a social worker who took in foster kids. Dilated cardiomyopathy, very advanced, had been on the transplant floor longer than anyone. I gave her a new heart on Thanksgiving. It failed today. She died before we could do anything."

As she talks, I lay the spinach on the omelet, sprinkle cheese on top, fold it over, and slide it onto the plate that I set in front of her. "I'm sorry."

"Thank you." She takes a bite, even though it just came out of the sizzling pan. "This tastes pretty good. I hope you're making one for yourself." She eats automatically, the same number of chews per bite, the same number of seconds between swallows until the omelet is gone and her gas tank is fueled.

We're not yelling at each other. We're not looking for the sharpest knives to hurt each other with. This is good.

There is no dancing around the question. I throw in it the hot pan to see what will happen.

"Did Cassie die like your patient?" I ask. "Did her heart fail?"

"I'd rather not talk about that with you," Mom says. "Not right now."

"But you saw the autopsy report, didn't you?"

"I don't think this is the right time—" Her beeper

vibrates on the table. "Damn." She reads the message, punches a number into the phone. "This is Doctor Marrigan."

I burn my fingertips pulling the muffins out of the oven. ~~They want to jump into my mouth. No, they want to roll themselves in butter and honey and jump into my mouth, one, two, three, four. And then some Moose Tracks ice cream and then some graham crackers and a jar of chocolate frosting and three bags of popcorn.~~

Dr. Marrigan gives orders about meds and drips and tests, then hangs up. "Are the muffins done?"

"A little hot."

"That's okay."

I pick up the dirty omelet plate and set three muffins in front of her. "You said that you were going to explain the autopsy results to Mrs. Parrish."

"I did."

"So what happened?

"Aren't you going to eat anything?"

I set the dirty plate in the sink. "I'm not hungry."

Mom peels the pink paper skin off the muffin. "What did you have for lunch?"

"I haven't eaten lunch yet."

"It's almost two o'clock. Have a muffin."

"I don't want one."

"And eggs. You could use the protein."

"I had milk in my cereal this morning."

"You need to eat." The Voice is back, giving orders, demanding obedience.

"Mom—"

The beeper signals again, bouncing around the table like an angry bee. "Dammit." She makes the call. "Dr. Marrigan."

I put the frying pan and the muffin tin in the sink, turn on the hot water and pour in the soap. The heat from the kitchen has fogged over the windows.

The real girl I was slips out and listens to the echo-voices shouting ugly at each other in every room of this house. Mom vs. Dad. Dad vs. Mom. Dad vs. Mom's job. Mom vs. Dad's girlfriends. MomDad vs. Lia's report cards, Lia's recitals, Lia's decision to quit again. Lia vs. everythingbody.

The voices slipped into this girl's mouth when she wasn't looking, like a bug on a summer's night that claws at the inside of your throat right after you realize you swallowed it. The voices swam around her insides and multiplied—charred, tinny echovoices that made a permanent home inside the eggshell of her skull.

::Stupid/ugly/stupid/bitch/stupid/fat/
stupid/baby/stupid/loser/stupid/lost::

"I said, 'Lia, look at me!'" Mom shouts, shaking my shoulders.

I blink. The dishes are done, but my hands are still in the sink. The bubbles are gone. The water is cold.

Mom ~~drags~~ guides me to her chair, one arm around my shoulders, the other reaching to take my pulse. She kneels in front of me and makes me look up, to the side, then straight at the light shining out of her pen.

"I bet your blood sugar is in the toilet," she mutters.

Three empty muffin papers are folded into triangles on her plate. A pale green pad of paper sits next to the plate, covered with her notes from the phone calls she took while I was in zombieland. Her juice glass and coffee cup are both empty. The water in the sink sucked time out of the room.

I lost ten minutes, maybe fifteen.

She pours me a glass of orange juice. "Drink this."

If I don't, there's a good chance she'll wrestle me to the floor, pry open my mouth, and pour it into me. Or drive me to the hospital and stick me with IVs until I inflate and bounce along the ceiling like a Thanksgiving Day parade balloon.

I gulp down the orange juice, pushing it to my stomach.

She sits, staring at me, as the fog clears from the windows and the battery acid spills into my veins.

"I'm okay," I say. "I'm just sad about Cassie."

Instead of answering, she gets up, slams the clean frying pan on the stove, turns on the heat, throws butter in the pan, yanks open the refrigerator door, takes out the eggs and milk, cracks two eggs in the pan, splashes milk on them, and beats it all with a fork.

"I'm not eating that," I say.

She hunches over the stove, scrambling, scrambling.

"I can't."

No response. Scramblescramblescramble.

"You aren't supposed to push me. I have to feel safe with food."

"That is the stupidest thing I have ever heard." She dumps the cooked eggs on a clean plate along with two muffins, stalks across the kitchen and puts it in front of me.

The orange juice is a virus attacking my insides. "Forget it."

She shakes her head. "You are not thinking clearly. You're dizzy. And you lied to me about breakfast."

"Okay, so I forgot breakfast. It's been a rough day."

"You look terrible. How much do you weigh?"

"Jennifer's the scale Nazi," I say. "Ask her."

She crosses her arms over her chest.

"Hundred and seven on Tuesday."

"I don't believe it."

"She'll show you the notebook."

"You're going to eat everything on that plate."

Two scrambled eggs + milk + butter = 365 + (two muffins = 450) = horror.

"I'll try."

I take a small bite of yellow. The orange juice is burning holes through the lining of my gut. I swallow yellow and grease, pick up another forkful and open wide for the airplane buzzing into the hangar.

Mom pours herself another cup of coffee.

I put the fork down. "I feel sick. I can't do this."

"You are sick. When you eat like a regular person, you'll feel better."

"Eating makes me feel worse."

"Take a bite of muffin."

I slowly peel off the pink paper. What was I thinking, cooking for her, trying to kiss Mommy's ouchie and make it all better? I cut the muffin in half, then one of the halves into four pieces, and each of those into two. I put one of the pieces in my mouth. A dry bubble of unmixed flour explodes on my tongue.

She watches me chew and swallow. She watches me not take another bite, *one minute, two, three, four* . . . Couple of years ago I saw Mom's tax return and I did the math to figure out her hourly rate. I just wasted twelve dollars of her time.

I push the plate away. "I can't."

Instead of exploding, she takes a deep breath and pushes the plate back toward me. "I'll make you a deal."

The orange juice is cramping my stomach. "What do you mean?"

"If you eat, I'll explain how Cassie died," she says.

"You're joking."

"Do I joke with you about food?"

~~I am so hungry~~ I have to stay strong—bend, but not break. "One muffin."

"Two muffins. You need the carbs."

"One and the eggs."

She takes another deep breath. "Deal."

It takes an hour.

Scrambled eggs = 25 bites.

One muffin = 16 bites.

◀ 036.00 ▶

My pink mouse stomach likes to be small and empty. It hates me for shoving in all that food. I lie down on the couch, pull the electric blanket over me, and try not to heave.

Mom perches on the couch opposite me. She pulls an afghan over her legs, the one I knitted last Christmas, full of dropped stitches and broken patterns. "You're sure you want to hear this."

"It can't be worse than what I've been imagining."

"It's ugly."

"Was she high?"

"No, nothing illegal, but she was on two antidepressants, a mood stabilizer, and ulcer medicine. And vodka. Lots of vodka."

"Alcohol poisoning?"

"No." She adjusts the pillow behind her back but doesn't say anything else.

"You promised," I say. "I did what you asked. You have to tell me. Everything."

"Everything?" She takes a breath and shifts into attending-physician mode. "Cassie had liver damage, her salivary glands were a wreck, and her stomach was distended." Mom holds up a loose fist. "A healthy stomach is this big. It can stretch to hold about a quart. Cassie's could hold three. Plus her stomach walls had thinned and were showing early signs of necrosis."

The last time I saw Cassie was just before Thanksgiving break. I was on my way to the library; she was putting up posters for the musical. Her outside was clean and colorful: new jeans, cute sweater, great earrings. Her cheeks were chipmunky and her hair looked like straw. She was not necrotic. She was chewing bubble gum. Her eyes were tired, but we're seniors. All seniors have dead eyes.

I walked past her and I whisperedsaid hello, but she didn't hear me.

Stretching and retching and filling up and emptying, the Cassie bucket was *dragged to the well over and over.*

"Cassandra had a terrible fight with her parents on Thursday, at Thanksgiving dinner," Mom says. "She got up to purge halfway through the meal. Cindy said even Jerry could see that she was back to her old habits. They told her she needed to go inpatient. She refused. She was nineteen, they couldn't force her. Jerry lost his temper and said he wouldn't pay for college until she was healthy. Cassie took off. She called Cindy and said she'd come home on Saturday, that she was at a friend's house. She was at the motel. She drank, binged, and purged for two days."

"So it was a heart attack? Because her electrolytes were messed up?"

Mom pulls the afghan up to her chest. "No, honey. Cassie's esophagus ruptured."

"Ruptured."

"Ripped open. Boerhaave's syndrome, usually seen in alcoholics who regularly upchuck after drinking too much. Vomiting forcefully enough can tear the esophagus." Mom looks down at her hands. "She was purging into the motel toilet when the rupture occurred. She was also, like I said, very, very drunk. She went into shock and died in the bathroom."

I count to ten, then to one hundred. Mom waits, watching. Inhale. Exhale.

"Do you have any questions?" she finally asks.

"Will it be in the newspaper?"

Mom shakes her head. "I doubt it. Since there were no drugs involved, they'll say something like the death was the result of a preexisting medical condition."

Out on the street, people are getting back into their cars, locking the doors, and driving away as fast as they can. If I were Mrs. Parrish, I wouldn't let them leave. I'd beg them to move in for a couple months, or pay strangers to occupy every room, eat my food, mess up my carpets, just so the house wouldn't be empty.

"Did she feel anything?"

Mom turns on the lamp on the table next to her. The storm has come down from the mountains. "I'm afraid she did. She died in terror and she died alone. It is an awful way to go."

I am an iceberg drifting toward the edge of the map.

"I don't believe you," I say. "You're making this up to scare me."

"I don't need to make anything up. She's dead, you went to her funeral. Cindy will show you the autopsy report, if you want."

"I don't want to talk anymore."

Mom leans forward. "You're allowed to feel upset about this. In fact, I'd rather see you upset than pretending it's not bothering you."

"You don't have to worry." I sit up and start to braid my hair. "I'm sad she died and I'm really sad she died in such a sucky way, but this is not going to ruin my life. Even before last summer Cassie and I weren't as close as when we were little."

We listen to the wind blow.

"Cindy wants to talk to you," Mom says. "She told

me you were the only person who could help her understand why."

"Why?"

She nods. "Cassie had everything: a family who loved her, friends, activities. Her mother wants to know why she threw it all away?"

Why? You want to know why?

Step into a tanning booth and fry yourself for two or three days. After your skin bubbles and peels off, roll in coarse salt, then pull on long underwear woven from spun glass and razor wire. Over that goes your regular clothes, as long as they are tight.

Smoke gunpowder and go to school to jump through hoops, sit up and beg, and roll over on command. Listen to the whispers that curl into your head at night, calling you ugly and fat and stupid and bitch and whore and worst of all "a disappointment." Puke and starve and cut and drink because you don't want to feel any of this. Puke and starve and cut and drink because you need an anesthetic and it works. For a while. But then the anesthetic turns into poison and by then it's too late because you are mainlining it now, straight into your soul. It is rotting you and you can't stop.

Look in a mirror and find a ghost. Hear every heartbeat scream that everysinglething is wrong with you.

"Why?" is the wrong question.

Ask "Why not?"

✳ ✳ ✳

The pager buzzes on the kitchen table. She swears, checks it, and makes the magic phone call. "Dr. Marrigan." After listening, she flies out of the room and up the stairs. I lie back down.

The blanket has finally heated up and I bury under it. My mouse tummy whimpers because she forced almost a thousand calories into me. I'll have to stay strong until dinner tomorrow to balance everything.

I drift away. . . .

"Lia, wake up." She shakes my shoulder again. "I have to go. The hospital." Her eyes are pointed in my direction, but she's seeing EKG readouts and blood-chemistry reports and the clean, smoking line she'll be cutting through her patient's chest in an hour or two.

I sit up, shivering, and reach for the controls of the blanket. "This thing isn't working."

"I unplugged it so you wouldn't get burned." She zips up her coat and bends over to kiss my cheek. "I'm sorry I have to go." She kisses the top of my head. "Get some rest."

She slams the door on her way out, but not because she's angry. Dr. Marrigan always slams doors to make sure they're closed tightly.

◀ 037.00 ▶

The house of my mother breathes and eats. The dishwasher cycles through RINSE, SCOUR, NORMAL WASH, ANTIBACTERIAL RINSE, and DRY. The heating system filters all the air through electrostatic lungs and exhales it with a hush. The hot-water tank fires up. The compressor of the refrigerator rattles, then hums, to keep everything cold.

It wouldn't matter if I screamed loud enough to break all of the windows. Everything would still function according to the owner's manual and guaranteed by a thick file of warranties.

I shiver across the floor and go to the bathroom. When I flush the toilet, the water whooshes everything out of sight. Before I crawl back under the blanket, I open the curtains and stand in front of the chilly French doors that overlook ~~what used to be heaven~~ the backyard.

When Dad left, she hired landscapers to turn the vegetable garden into a bed of perennials, something that she wouldn't have to fuss over or water much. The compost pile was taken away, the herb garden went to seed, and the special plot of the strawberry plants turned into a walkway. Guys came once a week to mow, trim, and rake.

I don't think she hired them this year. It must have been a jungle in July and August. Now it's a dead jungle.

The grass is knee-high and dead-brown, littered with the husks of weeds and fallen branches. The scraggly perennial bushes are choked with dry vines. The stump of the maple that used to hold up my tree house is rotting. It's like she doesn't even know she has a backyard.

. . . My tree house was our castle until the summer we were twelve.

Nanna Marrigan came to stay when school let out, because I was too old for a babysitter and too young to be on my own. She baked every morning: zucchini bread, oatmeal cookies, or blueberry pie. She taught me how to knit and Cassie how to crochet, the endless lengths of yarn spooling over her paper hands and around her crooked fingers.

We did not want to watch an old lady bake or knit. We wanted to hang out at the mall. We wanted to snap our fingers and turn sixteen so we could drive cars and have dangerous boyfriends. The tree house was too small for restless girls like us, but it was all we had. We read, played hearts and Uno, painted our nails, and ate Popsicles and cheese-and-mustard sandwiches until our shirts were permanently stained.

That was the summer I finally grew, after years of being smaller than everyone. Puberty stretched me on the rack until my arms and legs popped out of their sockets and my neck almost snapped. This new body smelled damp. The butt jiggled, the thighs looked a mile wide in

tights, and a soft double chin bubbled up. My ballet teacher pinched the extra inches, took away my solo, and told
me to stop eating maple-walnut ice cream. I went from
being the elegant swan to the ugly duckling that couldn't
walk without tripping over her own feet.

Cassie said ballet was for babies. I said I didn't really
care, though I did. Two days after that, she left for drama
camp and I was alone.

That was the summer my father's most famous book
was published and he was on the news all the time, and
Mom found out about his new girlfriend. He slept on the
couch for a couple of weeks, and then he moved out. Told
me he would always love me, no matter what, rented a
one-bedroom apartment, and left. Nanna Marrigan said
good riddance to bad rubbish, because she never liked my
dad to begin with.

Mom filed for divorce.

In the counselor's office, my parents claimed that we
would always be a family because of me, but things would
be better now. No more yelling, no more arguments. By
tearing our family apart, they were actually making it
stronger. By the time I figured out that they were not
making any sense, the family counseling was done and
Dad was walking down the aisle with Jennifer.

The growth spurt ripped my internal organs to
shreds. The pain woke me, screaming, almost every night.
My mother had me tested for twenty kinds of cancer and
consulted with experts who looked at the black-and-white

pictures of my insides and said nothing was wrong with me. The pain would go away when I stopped growing.

They lied, too. It got worse.

Nanna Marrigan headed home just before school started. Cassie came back from camp with a fake British accent, a nasty case of poison ivy, and three boxes of laxatives.

I showed her how I'd been making tiny cuts in my skin to let the badness and the pain leak out. They were shallow at first, and short, like claw marks made by a desperate cat that wanted to hide under the front porch. Cutting pain was a different flavor of hurt. It made it easier not to think about having *my body and my family and my life stolen, made it easier not to care. . . .*

Cassandra Jane's insides popped like a pink party balloon. Nobody sang to her or held her or helped her pick up the broken pieces. She died alone.

I can't let myself look out any of the windows that face her house, because it is only now beginning to sink in that she will never sleep there again, never slam the door, never sing in the shower when she's washing her hair.

I make my way back to the family room, eyes closed, feet shuffling across the floor. I don't let myself see anything until I am away from the dangerous windows.

My stomach is still whining, so I go back under the blanket on the couch, plugged in and turned to HIGH. The grease from the eggs mixes with the muffin dough and juice. It pours into my arteries, a slow-moving sludge that wants to turn into concrete. Any minute now my heart might just

stop.

◀ 038.00 ▶

I wake up more confused than usual because my bed isn't pointed in the right direction, only it's not even a bed, it's a couch, Mom's couch, the soft couch in the house of my mother. I am covered with a heavy Marrigan-woman quilt, patchworked with scraps of ancient dresses and weathered skirts.

I don't remember falling asleep or not being able to fall asleep or even dreaming. I didn't wake up when Mom came home. I can't tell if that's a good thing or a bad thing.

Cassie did not visit me last night. That's a good thing. Maybe she can finally sleep, too.

The air smells like it always does: coffee and bleach.

"Mom?" The word tastes funny.

"In here," she calls faintly.

I wrap the quilt around me and shuffle through the house. It feels like I've been gone for six lifetimes, not six months.

After Dad left, she changed everything: new furniture, new carpets, a totally new kitchen. She knocked down a couple of walls, redesigned the space on every floor, put in new windows, and moved the doors. We spent two years stepping over carpenters and masons and dust-covered guys who swore a lot. When it was over, she had a brand-new house, unstained by the presence of my father.

I half expected her to do it again after I left, but as far as I can tell only one thing has changed: all of the paintings and maps and photos of Maine and her grandparents and me as a ballerina, and me as a baby sleeping on her shoulder, all of them have been taken off the walls and set on the floor. They left ghosts behind, brightly colored rectangles with naked picture hooks and thin nails jutting out from the middle. The rest of the walls is faded.

Her voice filters through the closed library door. "I'll be out in a minute."

"I'll be upstairs."

My room is exactly the way I left it when they carted me off to New Seasons the last time, from the boot prints on the closet door to the shredded birthday cards on the floor. She didn't send in the cleaning lady to make my bed or haul it to the curb or vacuum or dust.

The door frame still has the pencil marks showing how much I grew every year after we moved in, up until I went to high school. Here is the one different thing: the frame has been painted with a clear coating, protecting the lines and the dates from being accidentally erased.

"Lia? Breakfast."
"Coming."

By the time I make it to the kitchen, she's pouring herself a bowl of granola. The counter is covered with food: cereal boxes, oatmeal packets, loaf of bread, bananas, the egg carton, cartons of yogurt, bags of bagels and doughnuts. She went shopping when I was asleep.

We look at each other over the food. Neither one of us say a word, but the old script is hanging in the air:

youhavetoeat/I'mnothungry/eatsomething/
stopforcing/listentome/leavemealone

Across the street, Mrs. Parrish is walking through a daughterless house, a Cassieless kitchen.

~~The doughnutsbagels smell heavenly plus sugar and I know what one taste would do~~ I have to eat a little of something or she'll go nuts and I am too tired to deal with it. I pick up the loaf of bread. "This doesn't have high-fructose corn syrup, does it?" I ask.

"Of course not," she says, pouring soy milk in her bowl. Her eyes widen a little as I take out a slice (77) and put it in the toaster.

"Is there any of Nanna's strawberry jam left?"

"I threw it out. Didn't trust the seals after so many years. I bought some plum preserves and honey."

Eating plain toast will detonate her. "I'll have some honey."

When the bread is done I scrape on a microscopic layer (30) of it and pour a cup of coffee, black. She pretends not to listen or watch as I crunch through my breakfast. I pretend that I don't notice her pretending.

"Why are all the pictures on the floor?" I ask.

"I've been meaning to paint, but can't decide on the color," she says. "It's been months. I should just hang them back up."

We have nothing else to talk about. Thank God for the newspaper.

After the dishes are washed, I shower and brush my teeth, not letting my eyes stray to the mirrors. I dress as slow as I can and pray that there will be a natural disaster that requires all doctors to go to the hospital for the rest of the day.

"Lia?" she calls. "Aren't you coming back down?"

She's waiting in the family room. When I walk in, hair dripping down my back, she pats the couch cushion next to her, once, like she isn't sure if she means it or not.

I sit on the other couch, the one with the electric blanket.

"So," she says. "What would you like to do?"

"I don't know. What do you want to do?"

"We could talk."

I should have gone back to bed. "Okay."

"How's school?"

"It sucks."

She leans forward to straighten the journals on the table between us. "Have you turned in your application yet? Taken the campus tour at the college?"

"I don't need a tour. I've been hanging around there since I was a baby."

"It might give you a new perspective. You could meet the person who leads the tours, make a couple of new friends. It might help with your motivation."

And so it begins.

I throw off the blanket and stand up. "This is stupid. You're going to lecture me and boss me around, I'm going to yell back, it'll be like always. We can't even pretend to get along. I'm out of here."

She puts up both hands. "Wait. I'm sorry. No lectures, I promise. Just a few more minutes, please?"

I sit and stare at my feet.

"When you lived here," she continues, "and you visited your father on the weekends, what did you do with him?"

"We mostly went to bookstores and read. Sometimes he'd take me to play squash."

"Do you like playing squash?"

"No. It's a horrible game."

"Why did you go with him?"

"It made him happy." I wait for her to recite everything that is wrong with Professor Overbrook, the catalog of his flaws and bad habits, and irritating gestures, but she doesn't. She is staring at my feet, too. She looks lost.

I sit back down. "Can we watch TV?"

"Good idea." She picks up the remote and points it.

We watch the Discovery Channel all morning. It's better than talking, but it's not as good as sprinting out the front door.

She does not comment on my lunch of lettuce and cucumbers. I don't say anything when she disappears into her computer for most of the afternoon.

The fight simmers gently on the back of the stove all afternoon, the bubbles rising up and popping, ingredients falling to the bottom, then surfacing again. It doesn't boil over until the sun sets.

Mom decides we're having sushi for dinner. I decide I'm not going with her to pick it up. She decides we're eating at the dining room table, because when things are formal, she's in control. I decide to read while I'm eating. She decides that I will eat four pieces of sushi and four pieces of sashimi and a bowl of udon noodles and tempura-fried shrimp. I decide that I'm not hungry. I drink green tea in a cup without a handle.

She doesn't push me to eat, so I know something's up. She waits until her plate is empty to drop the bomb. "I want you to move back here."

"No."

"You made good progress at your father's for a while," she continues, "but that seems to have stopped."

The floor rustles under my chair and vines grow up between the polished oak planks. I do not want to talk about this or listen to her talk about this.

She continues her speech. She must have worked on it for days. "I don't expect to be invited back to your therapy sessions. What goes on there is between you and Dr. Parker. But I think this would be a healthier environment right now."

I grow the vines up the legs of my chair and weave them into a tight spiral around me until they reach the ceiling. I can barely see her through the thorns. They block out most of her words, letting me drift off into a half sleep. A sharp question brings me back.

"How about next weekend?"

"What?"

"To move your things back here. Next weekend. I've already scheduled it off."

"I'm not moving back."

I need a diversion. I force my hand through the vines, pick up a piece of sushi and shove it in my mouth, swallowing it without tasting. The only way out of this is to play normal.

"What about every other week?" she asks.

"No."

"Why not?"

"Because I don't want to. I don't need to. Look, I'm

eating. I'm healthy. I'm normal. If anything, coming back here will trigger me. This is where I lived when it all started. Cassie's house is right across the street."

My brain (NO!) and stomach (NO!) scream at me (NO! NO! NO!) but I force a spoonful of noodles past my teeth and swallow.

"How about we just try a short test—a week?" she suggests. "You could come for Christmas break and go back to your father's when school starts in January."

"The whole break?"

Her mask slips and her shoulders slump. "Do you hate me that much?" she asks in a raw voice. "You can't even spend a week of your vacation here?"

The noodles stop halfway down my throat. "We can barely be in the same room for an hour, Mom. What would we do for a week?"

"I could teach you to play bridge," she says.

"I'd rather learn poker."

"I'll have one of my interns show me how to play. So you'll come for the break?"

~~No, I am never setting foot in this house again it scares me and makes me sad and I wish you could be a mom whose eyes worked but I don't think you can.~~ "Sure."

She smiles. "Thank you, Lia. That's a start."

Her eyes well up with tears and I cannot be in this room anymore.

I stand up. "Can I use your computer? I have home-work."

"Sure. The password is—"

"*Lia*. I remember."

I spend fifteen minutes Googling Cassie's name and checking local news sites to see if they've run any more stories about her. They haven't.

My fingers reach through the screen and comb through the garbage until they find the home of the shrieking chorus, hungry girls singing endless anthems while our throats bleed and rust and fill up with loneliness. I could scroll through these songs for the rest of my life and never find the beginning.

❁ ❁ ❁

i need some inspiration

❁ ❁ ❁

❁ ❁ ❁

I need a text buddy for fasting tomorrow. . . .

Please help!!!

❁ ❁ ❁

❁ ❁ ❁

good luck today beauties, you're strong

and will make today amazing

❁ ❁ ❁

❁ ❁ ❁

yeah i feel gross right now . . . only ate a bowl

of cereal today which is good

❀ ❀ ❀

if I eat that I'll have to run to get rid of it,

but I'm too tired to run

ever felt like this?

❀ ❀ ❀

The blogs and chat rooms are always filled with the buzzing of tiny wings, flies beating themselves against the inside of the monitor, not knowing why they're trying to escape. It will never change.

I type in the address of Cassie's secret blog. She stopped adding to it after she freaked out last summer, but she didn't delete it. I wonder if she stared at it as much as I do.

The Internet beams through me like I'm a paper bag, waves a magic wand, and *flash*, the pictures of two girls

flash waving from a tree house, lips stained grape-Popsicle

flash wearing identical bathing suits

flash eighth-grade Christmas break at Killington, the Christmas Dad went on his honeymoon, the Christmas Mom had hardwood installed in the whole house, the Christmas I refused to go with her to visit a new hospital in Costa Rica, the Christmas the Parrishes took pity on me and loaded my suitcase in the car for the drive to Vermont. I brought a backpack loaded with Tamora Pierce books, a small knife, and vodka stolen from Mom's liquor cabinet.

We skied for a week and a day. Cassie and I were eighth grade going on twenty-five, all grown up with lift passes and practically our own apartment, a mini-suite next to her parents in the time-share condo. We flirted with the guys working the lifts and pretended they flirted back. We obsessed about which bathing suits to wear to the hot tub and wrote down the calories in every bite of food.

flash us taking our own picture, cheeks sucked in

flash us comparing the size of our butts

For New Year's Eve, her parents gave us a bottle of alcohol-free champagne. After they left for the party at the lodge ("Don't let anyone in, girls, we're trusting you") Cassie mixed it with my vodka. We ate homemade gingerbread cookies and drank until our heads floated out the door, down the stairs, and into the frozen night.

The fingernail of a new moon watched us stumble across the bunny hill behind the condo. We made snow angels and tried to blow smoke rings with our smoky breath. Cassie got on all fours like a wolf and howled at the moon, eyes glittering. I made a bad wolf. I couldn't stop giggling. She howled louder and wilder, trying to bring real wolves out of the woods, or at least ski-lift operators, until somebody opened a window and told her to shut up. We collapsed in the snow, laughing.

Fireworks exploded overhead. Bells rang. Strangers shouted in one voice because it was New Year's and everyone was given a fresh start.

"We have to make resolutions," I said. "I resolve to read a book a day all year."

"That's stupid," Cassie said. "You already do that."

"So what's yours?"

She thought about it. "Resolutions are lame. I want to swear an oath."

"I swear to go back inside because I'm freezing my butt off."

"No, listen." She sat up and grabbed my arms. "It's midnight, it's a magic time. Anything we swear tonight will come true."

This was third-fourth-fifth-grade Cassie, the girl strong enough to punch boys and crazy enough to throw up in the roses. I would have followed her into a pit of fire.

We got on our knees.

"I swear that I will always do exactly what I want." She offered her hands up to the moon. "I will be happy and rich and skinny and hot. So hot the boys will beg."

I giggled again.

"Stop it," she hissed. "Your turn. Think before you open your mouth."

I would never be popular. I didn't want to be; I liked being shy. I'd never be the smartest or the hottest or the happiest. By eighth grade, you start to figure out your limits. But there was one thing I was really good at.

I took the knife out of my pocket and cut my palm,

just a little. "I swear to be the skinniest girl in school, skinnier than you."

Cassie's eyes got big as the blood pooled in my hand. She grabbed the knife and slashed her palm. "I bet I'll be skinnier than you."

"No, don't make it a bet. Let's be skinniest together."

"Okay, but I'll be skinnier."

We rubbed our hands and mingled our blood because it was forbidden and dangerous. The stars whirled above us and the firecrackers blazed. The moon stood watch as *drops of blood fell, careless seeds that sizzled in the snow.*

flash first day of ninth grade, bad haircuts

flash tenth-grade prom pictures with seniors we couldn't stand

flash last year, cast party, Cassie, drunker than they knew, me watching from a corner.

My mother knocks gently and opens the door. "It's getting late. I put fresh sheets on your bed, in case you want to stay here tonight."

I keep my eyes on the screen, fingers screaming across the keys to delete my history. She can't see what I'm doing. She moves to the window and pulls the curtain to the side.

"Oh, no," she says. "That's not good."

I shut down the computer and join her. Across the street, Mrs. Parrish is sitting on the curb, rocking back and forth, her arms wrapped around her body, wearing a thin nightgown and ratty slippers on her feet.

"I'll take care of her," Mom says. "You should go to bed."

"I need to get back to Dad's," I say. "I wasn't planning on spending two nights. My stuff for school is there."

Mom leaves first, while I'm packing. I clean up the kitchen and start the dishwasher. Before I can escape, a bone-handled knife from Nanna Marrigan's good silverware chest slips into my purse.

My car doesn't die until I pull into Jennifer's driveway.

◀ 039.00 ▶

Driving with blinking red lights on the dashboard made the engine of my car seize up. Dead engines are an expensive mad-Daddy bad thing. I am thoughtless/irresponsible/ just plain stupid sometimes. When he hollers at me, a vein over his left eyebrow pops up and quivers. The roar of his thunder makes Emma run to her room, with Kora and Pluto right behind her. Jennifer tries to referee by asking Dad if he wants to go for a walk with her, but he blows her off and rages at me for another half hour.

I want to tell him that it's just a stupid car, but bits of me are scattered all over town: the graveyard, school, Cassie's room, the motel, and standing in front of the sink in my mother's kitchen. It takes too much energy to gather all the bits together, so I just sit there and watch him implode. It's not like he can punish me anymore. What's he going to do? Make me stay in my room? Take away my phone privileges?

I have to take the bus to school from now on.

Emma's soccer season ends and basketball begins. I practice with her in the driveway. She can dribble three times before the ball takes off. It's my job to fetch it back.

She talks constantly, never stopping to breathe: the kids in her class, her teacher's twitching eye, the fish sticks in the cafeteria, the smell of the bathroom, Winter Concert rehearsals. She wants to learn how to ski, ice-skate, and snowboard. Riding a snowmobile looks like fun, too. She wants me to convince Dad to buy one for us. She asks me if I believe in Santa and if Santa is the cousin of Jesus, because she thinks they're related but they sure don't look like it. When her teeth start to chatter from the cold, I make her hot chocolate from scratch. I am so strong that not even one grain of sugar lands on my tongue.

I need to record her voice babbling so I can listen to it when she's not around.

❄ ❄ ❄

Mrs. Parrish leaves a message for me on the house phone every day for two weeks. She wants/needs/demands/begs/requests/deserves/would give anything just to talk to me. For ten minutes. It is important/vital/critical/imperative/necessary/essential/crucial that I call her back. Once she says my mother should be there, too. The next time she says never mind about my mother, just as long as I call her back.

People at school are saying that Cassie died of a heroin overdose. I'm not sure if I should tell the truth. Is it better to be known as the girl who died with a needle in her arm, or the girl who broke herself by puking too hard?

The yearbook staff is having a huge fight about how much space to give to her memorial. The people who knew her think it should be a full page. The people who believe the rumors about how she died think a half page at most or maybe her parents should buy a quarter panel so Cassie's picture could be with the local hardware store, insurance agency, and florist.

I leave a message for Elijah every day for two weeks. I say I found the junkyard, but he doesn't call back. I bet he figured out what a mess I am, which is bad because I need him to tell me more about Cassie's last day. It might help me figure out how to make her go away.

She hasn't gone away. If anything, being buried has made her stronger and angrier.

Cassie opens her Pandora's box every night and hitches a ride to my room. She doesn't watch from the shadows anymore. She attacks. Once the sleeping pill straps my arms and legs down to the mattress, she opens my skull and rips out the wiring. She screams holes in my brain and pukes blood down my throat.

It's easier to skip the sleeping pill, wait until Dad and Jennifer are both snoring, and spend three or four hours on the stair-stepper. When I finally crawl into bed, my pillow smells like burnt sugar and cloves and ginger.

I am 098.00.

I am 097.00.

I sharpen Nanna Marrigan's pretty knife and hide it under my mattress, just in case. I am 096.50.

Some nights I don't sleep at all. After working out, I knit, stitch by stitch, music on my headphones, rocking back and forth. It started as a scarf last year, but then it grew wings when I wasn't paying attention and demanded to be called a shawl, which I did, and then, when it was buried in the basket, it multiplied and turned into a blanket of a hundred colors and a thousand stories. I don't use yarn from a store. I buy old sweaters from consignment shops, the older the better, and unravel them. There are countries of women in this scarf/shawl/blanket. Soon it will be big enough to keep me warm.

My mouth and tongue and belly have begun to plot against me. I doze off in my room and *bam!* I'm standing in front of the refrigerator, door open, hand reaching for the cream cheese. Or the butter. Or the leftover lasagna.

"Take a bite," the white light inside the refrigerator

tells me. "A tablespoon, a teaspoon. Heat up a plate of lasagna, slow, at forty percent power in the microwave, and then pop it in the oven, top rack, at four-hundred degrees until the cheese bubbles and the edges brown. Sit down with Jennifer's silver-plated fork and the bone-handled knife and carve off one square inch. Take a pill to slow down time—you're going to want to enjoy this. Fill your mouth with melting cheese and sausage and tomato sauce—summer fresh/short skirt/dancing tomato sauce—and a slab of pasta as thick as your tongue. Swallow. Light up the stars in your brain, electrify your body, buckle on your smile, and everybody will love you again."

If I thought I could stop after one bite, two at the most, I would. But I am 096.00, close to dangerland. One bite of lasagna would cause a revolution. One bite, ten bites, the whole tray would pour down my throat. And then I'd eat Oreos. And then I'd eat vanilla ice cream. And Bluberridazzlepops, the rest of the box. And then, just before I exploded, my stomach ripping open and all the food falling into my body cavity, blood flooding me, then I'd have to go to the secret box in my closet and take out the laxatives and die of humiliation in the bathroom.

I take out the pickle jar. One spear, kosher dill = 5.

Kora and Pluto follow me upstairs. I check the secret box—emergency laxatives and diuretics— just in case. I haven't used it in months. It's a good thing I checked, because the supplies are low. Must remember that.

When I lay down on my bed, the cats hop up. They curl into my hollow places and purr so deeply it echoes in my bones.

◀ 040.00 ▶

Must. Not. Eat. Must. Not. Eat.

Must. Not. Eat. Must. Not. Eat. Must. Not. Eat. Must.
Not. Eat. Must. Not. Eat. Must. Not. Eat. Must. Not. Eat.
Must. Not. Eat. Must. Not. Eat. Must. Not. Eat. Must.
Not. Eat. Must. Not. Eat. Must. Not. Eat. Must. Not. Eat.
Must. Not. Eat. Must. Not. Eat. Must. Not. Eat. Must.
Not. Eat. Must. Not. Eat. Must. Not. Eat. Must. Not. Eat.
Must. Not. Eat. Must. Not. Eat. Must. Not. Eat. Must.
Not. Eat. Must. Not. Eat. Must. Not. Eat. Must. Not. Eat.
Must. Not. Eat. Must. Not. Eat. Must. Not. Eat. Must.
Not. Eat. Must. Not. Eat. Must. Not. Eat. Must. Not. Eat.
Must. Not. Eat. Must. Not. Eat. Must. Not. Eat. Must.
Not. Eat. Must. Not. Eat. Must. Not. Eat. Must. Not. Eat.
Must. Not. Eat. Must. Not. Eat. Must. Not. Eat. Must.
Not. Eat. Must. Not. Eat. Must. Not. Eat. Must. Not. Eat.
Must. Not. Eat. Must. Not. Eat. Must. Not. Eat. Must.
Not. Eat. Must. Not. Eat. Must. Not. Eat. Must. Not. Eat.
Must. Not. Eat. Must. Not. Eat. Must. Not. Eat. Must.
Not. Eat. Must. Not. Eat. Must. Not. Eat. Must. Not. Eat.
Must. Not. Eat. Must. Not. Eat. Must. Not. Eat. Must.
Not. Eat. Must. Not. Eat. Must. Not. Eat. Must. Not. Eat.
Must. Not. Eat. Must. Not. Eat. Must. Not. Eat. Must.
Not. Eat. Must. Not. Eat. Must. Not. Eat. Must. Not. Eat.
Must. Not. Eat. Must. Not. Eat. Must. Not. Eat. Must.
Not. Eat. Must. Not. Eat. Must. Not. Eat. Must. Not.

Eat. Eat. Must. Not. Eat. **Must. Not. Eat.**

◀ 041.00 ▶

Dad has been dragging his feet about buying a Christmas tree. Jennifer snags one from a toothless guy selling homegrown Douglas firs out of the back of his pickup. The guy carries it into the house but won't screw it into the tree stand until she gives him another fifty dollars. When Dad brings Emma home from basketball practice, she shrieks so loud that half of the needles drop off.

Basketball is working out better than soccer. Jennifer's bank sponsors the team and she told the coach that if Emma didn't play enough, she'd pull the sponsorship and take the uniforms back. Emma does not know this. She thinks she's the starting center because she's so strong.

I'm in the zone: half a medium-sized bagel (75) for breakfast, an apple (82) for lunch, and whatever I have to eat at dinner (500–600) to stay out of trouble. ~~Mom~~ Dr. Marrigan e-mails Daddy and says that she'll be at the hospital from now until Christmas, but after that, she has a week off and I've agreed to stay with her. She CCs Jennifer and me on the message. When Jennifer asks me about it, I say I haven't made up my mind yet.

Now that winter is here (this is official, because there is a tree shedding needles in our living room) it's easier to hide under layers of long underwear and turtlenecks, bulky sweatshirts and puffy down padding. Just don't look at the girl behind the curtain. Her knees are wider than her thighs. Her elbows are wider than her arms.

Jennifer is getting suspicious of the scales. I perform surgery on the Blubber-O-Meter 3000 scale, tinkering with it until it shows that I weigh 104.50. She sighs heavily when she writes the number down.

"I'm really sorry," I say. "I'll try harder, I promise. Just don't be mad at me."

Jennifer reports the new number to Daddy. I am supposed to be in the shower, not eavesdropping halfway down the stairs.

"Yes, she's down a few pounds, but once you start your holiday baking, she won't be able to resist," he says.

"If she loses any more, she should have a physical. Even if we have to make a big stink about it, like say the only way we'll let her stay is if she does it."

"It won't come to that. Why don't you make a cheese-cake this weekend, with strawberries on top? She used to love that."

Adrenaline kicks in when you're starving. That's what nobody understands. Except for being hungry and cold, most of the time I feel like I can do anything. It gives me superhuman powers of smell and hearing. I can see what people are thinking, stay two steps ahead of them. I do enough homework to stay off the radar. Every night I climb thousands of steps into the sky to make me so ex-hausted that when I fall into bed, I don't notice Cassie.

Then suddenly it's morning and I leap on the hamster wheel and it starts all over again.

Five hundred calories a day is working. Truth = 094.00.

Another goal weight. W00t.

I should be diamond sparkly champagne shooting to the stars, but the loudspeaker between my ears crack-les on, full volume, with another goal: 085.00, 085.00, 085.00.

085.00 is dangerland. 085.00 is Fourth of July fire-works in a small metal box.

The second time they ~~locked me up~~ *admitted me* for my own good, my whole body, including my skin, my hair, my baby blue toenails, and all my teeth weighed 085.00: 010.00 pounds of fat, 075.00 pounds of everything else.

Wreaths of pus-colored fat were suffocating my thighs, my butt, and my belly, but they couldn't see them. They said my brain was shrinking. Electrical storms were lighting up the inside of my skull. My tired liver was packing her suitcase. My kidneys were lost in a sandstorm.

085.00 was not enough stuffing for a paper Lia girl.

085.00 was skin that wanted to shed.

085.00 was fluffy monkey hair growing all over to keep me warm.

They said I had to get fatter.

I told them my goal was 080.00 and if they wanted my respect, they'd better stop lying to me.

When my brain started working again I checked their math. Someone made a mistake because they didn't figure in the snakes in my head and the *thick shadows hiding inside the cage of my ribs.*

085.00 is possible. I've been there before, in dangerland, sweet buzzing high gingersmoke air, crafty trolls hiding under bridges.

But 085.00 makes me want 075.00. To get there I'll need to crack open my bones with a silver mallet and dig out my marrow with a long-handled spoon.

◀ 042.00 ▶

When the college semester ends, Dad flies to New York for some research at a historical society and to get away from all of the crazy women in his house. Jennifer takes Emma to a basketball game. I stay home to study. I burn 858 calories on the stair-stepper, my legs smoking, hair on fire.

When they get back, I've covered the family room with note cards and open textbooks. They don't notice, because Emma is in pain and Jennifer is on the edge of total meltdown. During warm-ups before the game, my ~~step~~sister tripped on her shoelaces, fell on the court, and broke her right arm. They've spent the last two hours in the ER and now the arm is a hot-pink cast, and Jennifer's mascara is a mess.

I hug Emma's good side and kiss the top of her head. "I know how you feel, Emmakins. I busted my arm in first grade when Dad took off my training wheels. I pedaled three feet and crashed. Hit the ground so hard I cracked the concrete. It'll heal quick, don't worry."

"This is a little more serious," Jennifer says. "She fractured her ulna and her radius."

"That's what a broken arm is," I say carefully. "A fracture of the ulna or the radius, or both. Those are the technical names for the bones in your forearm. Do you want to talk to my mom about this?"

"She's a cardiologist, what would she know?"

I open my mouth but decide it's not worth the energy.

"Clean off the couch, please," Jennifer says, her face in the refrigerator. "She needs to rest with her arm elevated."

I make an Emma-nest with soft blankies and pillows and Elephant, Bear, and Snail, the inner circle of stuffed friends. As Emma lies back, remote in her good hand, Jennifer hands me her car keys and her debit card. "I need you to go to the drugstore and pick up the prescription that the doctor phoned in," she says. "And get her some Popsicles—the kind with fruit juice, not corn syrup."

"I don't want Popsicles, I want chocolate," says the victim on the couch.

I am not sure if I weigh enough to press down on the accelerator. I am 093.50 and have a 1,500-calorie deficit for the day. If I total another car, they'll lock me up and throw away the key.

"Um, I'm feeling kind of queasy. I don't think driving is a good idea."

Jennifer reaches into the glass jar on the counter, pulls out an oatmeal raisin cookie the size of my head, and shoves it at me. "Can we take the spotlight off you for just one minute, Lia? Put some food in your mouth, quit whining, and go to the damn drugstore."

I chew the cookie in the driver's seat, the car still safely in PARK. This cookie has no calories. It is not food.

It is fuel—gas and oil so the engine doesn't seize. I choke down a quarter of it and shift into DRIVE.

The guy behind the pharmacy counter says they're backed up because of the stomach bug going around and Emma's medicine will take another ten or fifteen minutes. The store has so many Christmas decorations, there is barely room left for the body wash and cough drops. The music is playing a little too loud. Somehow they've figured out how to pipe in the smell of gingerbread cookies, too.

I can't find the laxatives and diuretics. They've moved everything. Aisle 4 is Santa's Toyland. Aisle 3 has a snowdrift on the floor. A real snowdrift.

I look around. Tired people are wandering in search of hemorrhoid cream and painkillers and mouthwash. Two ladies scuff right through the snow, sending puffs of it into the air without noticing. When it falls, it doesn't melt. Kind of expensive advertising for a drugstore, but people have been saying that Amoskeag is the new Boston. I guess this is what they're talking about.

Cassie enters Aisle 3. The dead Cassie.

"Hey," she says. "Bottom shelf. That's where you'll find them."

She's wearing a gray ski jacket over her blue dress and has her hair slicked back into a wet ponytail, like she just stepped out of a shower. The smell of ginger and cloves and burnt sugar is thick.

"Aren't you proud of me for figuring this out, how to follow you?" Her voice buzzes like dying flies are trapped in her throat.

I bend down to the bottom shelf. She's right. I grab two boxes of diuretics and three of laxatives. Any second now, she'll disappear because she's a hallucination.

I stand up. She is so close to me, I could smell her breath, if she were breathing.

"Go away," I whisper.

"Are you kidding me?" She kicks at the snow and it fills the aisle, screening out the rest of the store and muffling the blaring carols. The snowflakes hang in the air, not rising, not falling.

"You don't belong here," I say. "Go back."

She frowns, confused. "But I want to hang out. It took a lot of work to figure out how to do this, you know. It's not like it's easy to go back and forth."

I cover my ears. "Stop it."

The night hauntings make sense. I'm tired then, drugged up, and have no sugar in my blood. But in Aisle 3 of Binney's Drugs? Jennifer must have slipped something into that cookie. She's trying to make me psychward crazy so she can get rid of me.

Cassie leans against the shelf. "You should pick up some bleach. You need it to clean up after the moldy banana in the purse at the back of your closet. It's disgusting."

"You're not here. I'm not talking to you."

She tilts her head. "You really mean it, don't you? You don't believe you're seeing me."

I try to walk past her, but my boots are frozen in the drifting snow.

"What do I have to do to make you believe?" she asks.

"Aren't you supposed to be in heaven or something?"

"That's a little complicated."

"You're a figment of my imagination, or a hallucination caused by my meds or that damn cookie. You do not exist."

Her eyes flicker, like a light switch is turned off, then on again. "That really hurts my feelings."

"My sister needs her medicine. I have to go."

The light shifts and she fades a little. I can see the outline of the shelves behind her.

She puts her mouth up to my ear. "You're almost there, buddy. Stay strong."

I can't move. I can't run.

"I know how bad you feel. Trapped," she says. "It gets better, I promise. So much better."

She looks like she used to when she was begging me to go to the park with her so she couldn't accidentally on purpose run into the latest guy she had a crush on. I should close my eyes until she vanishes. I don't.

"What are you talking about?" I ask.

She wipes a snowflake off my cheek. "You're not dead, but you're not alive, either. You're a wintergirl, Lia-Lia, caught in between the worlds. You're a ghost with a beating heart. Soon you'll cross the border and be with me. I'm so stoked. I miss you wicked."

I pull back, try to shake the cobwebs out of my head. "What is wrong with you? Don't you care about what happened?"

She frowns.

"Don't you care that your parents have gone off the deep end? You shouldn't have done it. You should have asked for help."

The snow rushes toward her and spins in a whirlwind that reaches up through the ceiling.

"I tried." The flames in her eyes burn my cheeks. "You didn't answer the phone."

◀ 043.00 ▶

It didn't happen. I didn't see her. Everything is fine.

Fine. Fine. Fine. Fine. Fine.

I take the medicine home to Emma, eat a cup of tomato soup made with water (82) and pretend to finish my homework. While the two of them watch a movie, I run scalding water into the bathtub, strip, and get in.

The merry-go-round is spinning too fast. I want to get off. I want to close my eyes, or just blink. I want to choose what I see and what I don't see. The crap we put up with when we're awake every day—school, house, house, mall, world—is bad enough. Shouldn't I at least get a break when I'm asleep? Or, if I'm doomed to be haunted by ghosts, shouldn't they only work at night, and dissolve when hit by sunlight?

I lift my arm out of the water. It's a log. Put it back under and it blows up even bigger. People see the log and call it a twig. They yell at me because I can't see what they see. Nobody can explain to me why my eyes work different than theirs. Nobody can make it stop.

The merry-go-round spins again. To get off this thing I think I have to scream. But I can't. My bone corset is laced so tight, I can barely breathe.

When Cassie creeps into my bed that night and curls her hands around my throat, she doesn't bring up what did not happen at the drugstore. Neither do I.

My heart clangs like a fire bell all night long.

◀ 044.00 ▶

The show must go on.

There is no way a kid with a fractured ulna and radius can play the violin in the Park Street Elementary School Winter Holiday Concert, so the band director is rigging up a metal triangle that Emma can ting at the right moment. She's also in charge of the sleigh bells during "Jingle Bells." She spends all of Thursday night practicing.

I leave school early (cramps—ha) and spend Friday afternoon baking, because Emma signed her mother up to bring something to the Holiday Bake Sale, and Jennifer went out and bought cheap cookies with tacky red-and-green icing. I make gingerbread girls, each with a pink cast on her arm, and a loaf of Nanna Marrigan's date-nut bread. The measuring spoons want to stick sugar and butter and molasses into my mouth. I pretend I am allergic to the ingredients. One taste and my lips and tongue will swell up and I will choke to death.

I use the leftover gingerbread bits to make a voodoo cookie, a sturdy girl with yellow-red hair, a blue dress, and a black hole for a mouth. After she cools, I lay her on the cutting board and smash her with the rolling pin until she is a pile of gingerdust.

When Emma comes home from tutoring, she smells the cookies and shrieks so loud the rest of the needles fall off the Christmas tree. She throws her arm and her cast around me and squeezes, almost fracturing my ribs. I let her paint my fingernails the same color as hers so we can be twins.

Jennifer is a little stunned by the cookies. Emma reminds her that she signed up to work the bake sale and I offer to take her place, which surprises her even more.

We only have time for turkey sandwiches (230) before we have to leave for the concert.

✳ ✳ ✳

Park Street Elementary School smells exactly the same as it did when I went there: warm sweaty bodies, cheap spaghetti sauce, Magic Markers, and paper. There is a tribute to Cassie on the bulletin board in the front hall. The picture was taken a couple of years ago, before the puking burnt out her salivary glands and they swelled up into walnut-sized lumps at the back of her jaw. Seeing it makes my heart pound, but I keep walking, turn right at the library, left at the end of the hall. The picture really is there, I didn't make it up, it's not a ghostly vision. Her dad is the principal here and her mom runs everything else. It makes sense to erect a shrine.

Emma skips off to the backstage area to line up.

"You sure you don't want to come in and listen?" Jennifer asks me. "We could switch at intermission."

And sit with six hundred overheated parents all armed with video cameras? "No, really, you go ahead. Stay for the whole thing."

She hugs me, squeezing tight enough to make my ribs groan. It happened so quick I didn't see it coming. She lets go, grabs my face in both hands and kisses my nose. "You can be so sweet sometimes, you know that? I owe you huge." She leans close and whispers, "I can't stand those women. They make me scream."

"No problem," I say, trying not to stagger under the weight of her kiss.

There are four cafeteria tables set up in the back hall

for the bake sale. The tables are crowded with plates of cookies with ten kinds of chocolate chip, including wheat-, dairy-,and egg-free. The moms at this school watch way too many cooking shows. There are truffle brownies, cinnamon wafers, peppermint fudge. Someone baked cupcakes in bizarre flavors: pomegranate, green tea, cranberry, pistachio, and guava. (The cupcakes come with labels listing the ingredients for the allergic.) On the last table, near the cash box, are two buckets filled with chocolate-dipped pretzels rolled in jimmies, and three perfectly made gingerbread houses that are up for silent auction. One has stained-glass windows made out of melted candy.

The moms I'll be working with are shoving cookies into their mouths and letting the crumbs collect on their sweaters.

"Want some fudge?" they ask, staring at my collarbones. "Try the seven-layer bars. They're to die for."

I would love a seven-layer bar. I would love to pick up a piece of fudge, gossip about the latest episode of whatever, bite the fudge, laugh, chew it because it tastes good and it feels good in my mouth, and swallow and have my tummy glow with fudginess. But they are not for me.

"No, thank you," I say.

"Look at how skinny you are!" they shriek. "You don't have to worry, not like us!" They slap their thighs, wiggle their butts, pinch their bellies. "Take a piece. Take two!"

A hand above twitches my puppet strings. The corners of my mouth turn up and I bat my eyelashes, shrug my shoulders a little. "I had a huge dinner," I say. "I'll have something later."

A wave of hungry people interrupts us and we sell, sell, sell. At one point I see Mrs. Parrish, dressed as Mrs. Claus, drifting through the crowd. Her wig droops to one side. A group of little kids rush up to her and wave, asking her to tell Santa they've been very good this year. She walks by without noticing them, heading straight for the bake-sale table. I hide behind a gingerbread house until she's gone.

When the concert starts, I tell the fat moms to go listen to their kids, I'll guard the food and the cash box. This stuff doesn't tempt me. It makes me queasy; that's how strong I am.

The moms give me a hundred chances to change my mind ("No, I'm sure, really, you guys go ahead, honest, really"), then they hustle toward the auditorium armed with emergency brownies in case of an unexpected blood-sugar crash.

I sit behind the mountain of individually wrapped marshmallow treats. The band is playing either "Silent Night" or "It Came Upon a Midnight Clear." I scan up and down the hall. Cassie has not popped up, not yet. There's no snow in sight. It does smell like gingerbread, but that's because of the bake sale. I don't think she's coming, not with her face stapled to the bulletin board like a WANTED poster, not with her parents here. They'd see her, too, I know it. All hell would break loose. She wouldn't dare.

I take out my knitting, hold the needles tightly, and loop the yarn. Knit, knit, purl. Knit, knit, purl. The yarn is damp from the sweat on my hands. Knit, purl, knit. No. I back up and undo the stitches. Knit, knit, purl.

~~My traitor fingers want that fudge.~~ No, they don't. ~~They want a seven-layer bar and some weird muffins and those pretzels.~~ No, they do not. ~~They want to squish the marshmallows and stuff them into my mouth.~~ They will not.

The knitting sinks into my lap. The needles are too heavy, the yarn spun from iron. The cartilage in my fingers and knees and elbows is thinning. Hungryhungry battles starvestarve back and forth across the battlefield of my mind.

Everything hurts.

A door opens and closes and blows the smell of ginger and cloves and burnt sugar into my face and hair.

So far today, I am 412 calories. I'll burn that and a couple hundred more if I can find the energy to climb on the stair-stepper. I could eat half a cupcake (150), or a quarter (75). I could scrape off the frosting and just nibble at the cake.

I shouldn't. I can't. I don't deserve it. I'm a fat load and I disgust myself. I take up too much space already. I am an ugly, nasty hypocrite. I am trouble. I am a waste.

I want to go to sleep and not wake up, but I don't want

to die. I want to eat like a normal person eats, but I need to see my bones or I will hate myself even more and I might cut out my heart or take every pill that was ever made.

I take the cupcake guaranteed to taste the worst: pomegranate. It has pink frosting and red seeds on top. I lick off the seeds and bite. They explode in my mouth, wet-red tang, not like a berry, not like an apple, but darker, close to wine. I could eat a handful of these seeds, or six handfuls, or I could pour a bucket of them into me.

No, I couldn't. I just eat six seeds: 1.2.3.4.5.6. They feel warm going down my throat, not scary.

I hear a door open, but I can't see it. The puppet strings of this body are cut and I can't feel these hands, or stop them from peeling the paper wrapper off the cupcake and shoving it in me. This mouth chews and swallows and hurry because here comes another and another until all the red-seeded cupcakes are gone. Every. Single. One. These hands reach for a brownie next, and then a piece of fudge and a pink-armed gingerbread Emma girl. I dissolve into a spun sugar blur until the doors of the auditorium burst open and the hall fills with applause and whistles, and warm bodies.

I sprint to the bathroom.

It doesn't matter how far down I stick my finger, the cesspool won't empty. I squirt soap into my mouth instead and gargle until the bubbles stream down my cheeks.

◀ 045.00 ▶

In the middle of the night, someone thrusts a sword into my guts. I wake up screaming for my parents, but Jennifer rushes in because my father is off on another trip and my mother doesn't live here. She helps me drag myself to the bathroom. I can't tell if I should sit on the toilet or stick my head in it.

I drop my drawers and sit. Jennifer wets a washcloth with cold water, wrings it out, and puts it on the back of my neck.

"I'm okay," I mutter.

"You are not." She presses the back of her hand to my forehead. "No fever. Could be food poisoning, I think. What did you have for lunch?"

The blade rips through my belly again and I choke back a moan. "Soup and crackers. And we all ate the sliced turkey in our sandwiches for dinner."

"Are you nauseous?"

I shake my head.

"Did you eat anything at the bake sale?"

Before I can lie, my head bobs up and down. "Cupcakes."

"Cupcakes? You ate more than one?"

I nod again. "They tasted good."

"I can't see how a cupcake would do this to you. Maybe they used raw egg in the icing. Will you be okay if I go downstairs for a minute? I want to look something up."

"What?" I grit my teeth. "Sure. When you come back, can you bring me peppermint tea?"

"You shouldn't eat anything until your stomach settles."

"Please, Jennifer. I know it will help."

"All right, relax. Just breathe. Peppermint tea, coming up."

Once she's gone, I groan. I know exactly what's wrong. I am a gluttonous, gorging failure. A waste. My body isn't used to high-sugar carbs laced with witchcraft. It can barely cope with soup and crackers.

The blade twists again. The laxatives I wolfed down when we got home are torching my guts. Plus, my phosphate levels are out of whack because of the unexpected sugar. Plus, there is a chance that I have been so gifted at starving myself that the empty string balloon of my guts is turning from pink to ghost gray as the cells die off from neglect. Or Cassie has made a gingerbread voodoo doll of me on her side of the grave and is stabbing it into bloody bits.

My head is too heavy to sit on my shoulders. I bend over and let it dangle between my legs.

"Lia?"

Through the curtain of my hair I watch Emma's slippers shuffle into the bathroom. "Lia, are you going to die?" Tears are perched on the edge of her voice.

I force myself upright and try to ignore the black spots opening up in front of my eyes.

"I just have a tummy ache, honey. Nobody dies from that. I'll be fine."

Jennifer takes Emma back to bed and chooses to believe my lie about how I'm feeling much better and how I'm going to read on the toilet for a while, just in case. I spend most of the night shuffling between my bed and the toilet, emptying, emptying, emptying as the laxatives grind through me and do their dirty work. I scrub the toilet with the blue cleaner after every trip.

When I fall into bed, somebody starts beating on my chest with a baseball bat. I try to take my pulse, but my heart is hammering too fast to count. I'm sweating. My body is eating itself, chopping up my muscles and throwing them in the fire so the engine doesn't seize.

There is metal in my mouth. I need to wake up Jennifer.

If I wake her up, she'll freak.

If she freaks, she'll call an ambulance.

If the ambulance comes, I'm doomed.

I roll over and ask Cassie to rub my back and sing to me.

◀ 046.00 ▶

When Dad comes home from New York City on Saturday, I'm dozing on the couch. He shakes my shoulder and I jump, not sure where I am or who I am or who he is. He doesn't notice.

"Where are Jen and Emma?" he asks.

I sit up. Slowly. The worst cramps from last night are gone, but it feels like I did a hundred thousand crunches suspended upside down. "The mall. How was your trip?"

"Excellent," he says. "My editor is extending the deadline and she's giving me another advance to pay for a research trip to London. I am The Man."

He tries to pump his fist in the air like he's a pro football player, but he looks more like a lame college professor trying to hail a cab.

"That's great, Dad."

His smile fades. "Are you okay? You don't look so hot."

"I had food poisoning last night, from a cupcake." I pull the blanket around my shoulders. "Go figure."

"Did you call your mother?"

"No."

"She is a doctor, you know."

"Yes, I am aware of that. I didn't need her to charge over here with an ambulance in the middle of the night. Jennifer helped me. I'm fine, just tired."

"Are you sure?" He lays the back of his hand on my forehead.

"Why are you doing that?"

"It's what you do when your kids are sick."

"You're hopeless," I say.

He gives me a quick hug. "In the best possible way. I brought you girls some presents from the city, maybe that will help. Hang on."

He leaves the room and comes back with a plastic bag. "Take a look."

I empty the bag. I'm guessing that the magic wand filled with sparkles is for Emma, which means the books are for me: all stories about the agony of middle school, written for twelve-year-olds. Unless the books are for Emma and the wand is for me. That could be useful.

"Do you want strawberry, grape, or honey?" Dad asks as he walks into the kitchen.

"What?"

"Strawberry, grape, or honey? It's almost lunch—I'll make us peanut butter sandwiches."

I tuck the magic wand under my arm and follow him, blanket trailing behind me like a cape. "I'm not hungry. My stomach is still off."

"I'll make tea and toast instead. Have you taken your meds?"

My head shakes "no" before I can stop it.

"That settles it. You need to have something in your

stomach and then you can take your medicine. Have a seat, kiddo."

While the bread for me is toasting (2 slices = 154), he makes two sandwiches for himself, both with crunchy peanut butter and grape. He sticks a mug in the microwave for the tea and absently takes a bite of one of the sandwiches. He gets a plate out for my toast and takes a second bite. He just eats and goes about his business, buttering the toast (100) without asking me, getting the milk out of the fridge and carrying it to the table with the plate and tea. Half of his first sandwich is already gone.

How does he do it?

I can't remember what it's like to eat without planning for it, charting the calories and the fat content and measuring my hips and thighs to see if I deserve it and usually deciding no, I don't deserve it, so I bite my tongue until it bleeds and I wire my jaw shut with lies and excuses while a blind tapeworm wraps itself around my windpipe, snuffling and poking for a wet opening to my brain.

I am so tired. I have forgotten how to sleep, too.

Dad blathers on about a bunch of moldy letters in the London archives and how if we get a good deal on the tickets, we could all go to England, which will never happen. I swallow my pills and drink my tea. Just as I reach for half a slice of bread (38) + quarter tablespoon butter (25) = 63, the phone rings.

I start to get up.

"Don't," he says. "Let the machine answer."

After the beep, Mrs. Parrish's voice crackles on the speaker. "Lia? Lia, please call me back. I'm not angry, I promise. We've looked everywhere and we can't find Cassie's necklace, the one with the silver bell. I thought maybe if I wore it . . . Can you help me?" Her voice breaks and she sobs once, then sniffs. "I just want you to call me, Lia. I can't . . . I need you to help."

After she hangs up, Dad erases the message. "She should be talking to her therapist instead of bothering you."

I study the cracks in the grout between the floor tiles. If I could turn into a wisp of smoke, I could slip into them and disappear.

"It's okay," I lie. "She's stuck. It's sad."

"Is that how you feel, too?" He sips his milk. "Stuck and sad?"

I should have pretended to stay asleep when he came in. "No."

"That's what it looks like to us."

"Who is 'us'?"

The peanut butter tries to glue his mouth closed, but it's not strong enough. "I had a long talk with your mother last night."

"You talked to Mom twice in one year?"

"No sarcasm, please." He takes another bite of his sandwich and chews. "Chloe thinks you should be evaluated."

"Evaluated?"

"Jennifer does, too."

"Evaluated for what?"

He stops eating. "To see if you should go back to the hospital as an inpatient."

The cracks in the floor open wider. "You want to lock me up again?"

"Chloe said she was going to call this morning and talk to you about this."

"She didn't." I shiver. The cold is soaking through the windows. "Do you think I should go back?"

"Honestly? It seems a little extreme. Your grades could be better, but you go to school. You don't sneak off at night and get into trouble. I'd like you to put some weight back on. I told your mother that going back to the nutritionist for a few visits would probably be enough."

"But Mom wants to lock me up."

"The evaluation could prove her wrong—think of it that way."

"She's already scheduled the appointment, hasn't she?"

He picks up the magic wand and tilts it so the sparkles run down the inside, perfectly sealed in plastic. "Ten o'clock, two days after Christmas."

The cracks in the floor gape open, bottomless stone canyons. I teeter on the edge.

"Lovely," I say. "I'll be able to write an essay about my Christmas vacation on the feeding farm where they stuffed tubes up my nose and made me eat butter and gave me pretty little pills and then they vacuumed out my brain and turned me into a fat zombie. What fun."

"You won't be admitted unless you really need it. Don't you want to be healthy, to feel better?"

"You're just trying to get rid of me."

"I'm worried about you. I want my little girl back."

I stand up and pace between the table and the stove. "I tried the hospital. Twice." The cape slips off my shoulders. "You said it was the last time because I used up all the insurance."

"If you have to go inpatient, your mother will sell some stock and I'll remortgage the house. But it doesn't have to come to that. If you'd just eat—"

"I don't need to eat like you."

"Dammit, Lia!" he yells. "That's not true and you know it. Are we supposed to let you starve yourself to death?"

That yelling-Daddy-voice used to scare me. Now it just makes me vicious. "Your wife watches me step on the stupid scale every week."

"And your weight is going down. This week was what, 104? You swore to me you'd stay at 110."

"I have a tiny frame and a fast metabolism."

"Again with the bull!" He sprays sandwich spittle across the table. "You begged me to let you move in. You couldn't live with your mother a minute longer. You said she was the problem and I believed you, just like I believed you when you promised to be honest."

I try to lower my voice. The more he loses control, the more I have to hold on to it. "You suck at promises, too. All those canceled weekends, the trips we were going to take, the house you said you'd buy on a lake."

He glares at me. "Don't change the subject."

"I need time, Dad," I say. "I just can't stick food in my mouth. I have to start my whole life over again."

"When will that happen, exactly?" His voice turns ugly as well as loud, the voice that used to fight with my mother when I was supposed to be sleeping. "Sometime this year? This century?"

"I'm working on it," I say.

"No, you're not. You've been here for six months and you haven't unpacked your damn boxes."

"Oh, you finally noticed?" I snarl back.

"What does that mean?" he asks.

"You're never around. Jennifer takes care of everything so you can go to your meetings and the library and your squash games and your fancy dinners. Oh, wait a minute—when have I seen this before? Got another girlfriend, Daddy? Ready for round two in divorce court? Don't forget to line up a good shrink for Emma; she thinks you're a god."

His face is the color of a heart attack. The muscles in his jaws are clenched so tight his teeth could crack. Any minute now, he's going to pick me up and throw me through a window and I won't touch the ground for a thousand miles or so.

He picks up the milk jug and pours more into his glass. He takes a long drink of milk and very deliberately sets the glass back on the table. "Stop turning this into an examination of my faults. We're talking about you, Lia."

The lines in his face sag with disappointment. His eyes are red-rimmed with long nights and too many mistakes and a defective daughter. It's easier to fight back when he yells.

"I wish I understood what goes on inside you." He tilts the magic wand again but doesn't look at the sparkles. "Why you're so afraid."

The merry-go-round spins inside my head, spins so fast all I can see are honey-yellow, strawberry-red, grape-purple splashes streaking past my eyes. I should never have come to this house, but I had nowhere else to go.

"Please, Lia." His voice has dropped to a whisper. "Please eat."

The merry-go-round snaps and splinters and bits of color fly through my head.

I snatch the sandwich on his plate and shove it in my mouth.

"Is this what you want?" I scream. "Look—Lia's eating! Lia's eating!" With every chew, I open my mouth wide so the bread and jelly and peanut butter and saliva spill into the canyons beneath us. "Are you happy now?"

He calls my name as I run out of the room.

He does not follow me.

◀ 047.00 ▶

I turn up the space heater in my room to the highest setting and crank the volume on my speakers as high as they
will go. The music liquefies the air and blows the papers
off my desk. I crawl into bed, but the mattress is stuffed
with stones and shells and I can't get comfortable. I open
books, but the stories are all locked up and I don't know
the magic words.

WhatWhyWhenHowWho? WhatWhyWhenHowWho?
WhatWhyWhenHowWho?

What am I afraid of? Why can't I even want to get
better? When am I me and how do I know that and who
would I be if I did what they want?

How did I get like this?

Maybe Mom took drugs when she was pregnant with
me. She started her residency that year—she probably
went the whole nine months without sleeping and I was
born with over-caffeinated-fetus syndrome. Or Professor Overbrook smoked weed laced with an experimental
chemical and he knocked up Mom with mutant sperm.

Whatever.

I dust my shelves and the windowsills and walk downstairs to get the vacuum cleaner, a glass of ice cubes (Professor Overbrook tries to talk to me, too bad he doesn't
exist, I don't have a father or a mother I just have white
spaces with no walls), and the box of garbage bags. Once

the carpet is sucked clean, I rip open one of the cardboard boxes packed full of my crap from Mom's and stuff it all into a garbage bag. Don't even look at it. Don't listen to my fingers telling me it's a doll, a necklace, a Jane Yolen paperback, a collection of coins. I crush ice between my teeth and swallow the slivers. Everything is garbage.

Professor Overbrook walks in as I'm tying off the third bag. I watch his mouth move. He hands me a mug of fresh-brewed peppermint tea and a plate of the ugly-iced cookies Jennifer bought for the bake sale. He is going to his office to pick up some source material he forgot.

After he runs away, I crumble the cookies into the toilet and flush. I slip some extra crazy candies into my mouth and wash them into me with ice water, then struggle through five hundred crunches—

::Stupid/ugly/stupid/bitch/stupid/fat/
stupid/baby/stupid/loser/stupid/lost::

—even though it hurts my belly. Especially because it hurts.

Lia the Loathsome calls the front desk of the Gateway. Lia the Loathsome tells the Charlie who answers the phone that if he doesn't get Elijah on the phone this minute, she'll call the police and report that Charlie sexually harassed her.

He says, "Hang on."

While I'm waiting, I scrape off my fingernail polish. Dr. StupidParker says that when I'm sad it really means I'm angry and when I'm angry it really means I'm afraid. I can't believe she gets paid for dreaming up crap like that. I feel like starting a war or blowing up a building or breaking every window in this house. I wonder what she'd say that really means.

Elijah finally picks up the phone. "Hey there. What's up?"

Lia: I have to talk to you.

Elijah: Are you Emma today or Lia?

Lia: You lie all the time.

Elijah: It's a bad habit.

Lia: I'm sorry. I apologize.

Elijah: Okay. No worries.

Lia: So, are we friends again?

Elijah: I guess.

Lia: Good. How's your car?

Elijah: It'll be ready by the time Charlie closes up for the winter.

Lia: Where're you going?

Elijah: Oxford, Mississippi, maybe. Or I might head back to Mexico. I liked it there. *(He covers the mouthpiece of phone, talks to Charlie.)* I have to go. Boss has this weird idea that I should actually work while he's paying me.

Lia: No, wait, I have a question.

Elijah: Shoot.

Lia: You said the first time you saw Cassie was when you found her body.

Elijah: That's not a question, but yeah.

Lia: At the cemetery you asked me why I didn't answer when she called that night. How did you know she called me?

Elijah the Silent:

Lia: Are you still there?

Elijah: Can we talk about this later?

Lia: No. You have to tell me. She wanted you to.

Elijah, after a deep breath: She checked in Thursday night, but I didn't run into her until Saturday. She invited me to hang out so I went to her room after work. She'd been drinking—a lot. I ate a couple cookies and decided things were not cool. I took off.

Lia: How do you know she called me?

Elijah: I played cards with Charlie until midnight and decided to go downtown. Cassie saw me walking by and opened the door, crying her eyes out and babbling about Lia being mad at her, Lia won't answer. I told her to sleep it off. She wouldn't leave me alone until I wrote down your phone number and promised to give you her message. I got out of there as fast as I could.

Lia: What did she say?

Elijah: I told all of this to the cops, you know. They watched the security tapes; it's a good thing Charlie's paranoid. I never touched her. I didn't even take her purse, though I could have. She showed up on the tape a couple hours after I left, staggering around the parking lot and singing to the moon. Then she went back inside.

Lia: What was the message?

Elijah: Nothing, really. Remember, she was trashed.

Lia: Tell me.

Elijah: She said, "Tell Lia she won. I lost and she won." That's the quote. It seemed real important at the time, but now it's kind of silly, I guess. Did you guys have a bet? What did you win?

I hang up the phone without saying good-bye.

I won the wintergirl trip over the border into dangerland.

◀ 048.00 ▶

I turn the music back up to SHATTER and head for the bathroom to brush the phone call and the dust and the sandwich out of my mouth.

1.2.3.4.5.6.7.8.9.10.11.12.13.14.15.16.17.18.19.

20.21.22.23.24.25.26.27.28.29.30.31.32.33.

I did not win. I can't believe she said that. Typical Cassie crap, melodramatic and over the top. It's not my fault she flipped out so easy or her parents never paid attention. It's not my fault she puked, or that puking was the only thing that made her feel better.

she called me.

I brush until my gums bleed, then I scrub harder. Red Lia juice dribbles down my chin, transforming me into a hungry vampire ready to suck the life out of anyone who pisses me off. Maybe that's my problem. Maybe I am one of the undead. Vampires are pale, cold, and skinny like me. They secretly hate the taste of blood, hate the way they make people cry, hate graveyards and coffins and the beast that drives them. They will lie about hating it until someone drives a stake through their heart.

. . . body alone . . .

I put my mouth under the tap, rinse and spit.

The scale shows up on the floor, the good one, the one that does not lie. I strip, stand on it, to weigh my faults and measure my sins.

089.00.

I could say I'm excited, but that would be a lie. The number doesn't matter. If I got down to 070.00, I'd want 065.00. If I weighed 010.00, I wouldn't be happy until I got down to 005.00. The only number that would ever be enough is 0. Zero pounds, zero life, size zero, double-zero, zero point. Zero in tennis is love. I finally get it.

I open up the window and throw the scale into the front yard. Turn on the shower; hot water only, stare into the mirror. The holes in my face are filled with sand and pus. The whites of my eyes are lemonade puddles spilled over with purple shadows lying under them. My nose is hair and snot, my ears are candle wax, my mouth is a sewer. I am locked into the mirror and there is no door out.

::Stupid/ugly/stupid/bitch/stupid/fat/
stupid/baby/stupid/loser/stupid/lost::

Nanna Marrigan's bone-handled knife slides out from under my mattress, slithers into the bathroom, and lies down to the left of the sink, blade facing the glass wall.

The pills I took an hour ago bang through my veins like metal trash cans blowing down the street. The snakes in my head wake up, slither down my brain stem, and snap at the dozing vultures. The birds flap their nightwings once, twice, three times, and circle high in the air. Their shadows blot out the sun.

I use my shirt to wipe the steam off the mirror. It's beading up on my arms, too, pearling on my lanugo fuzz, the little white hairs I've started growing to keep me warm.

Stupid body. What's the point of growing fur and letting the hair on my head fall out?

"Wouldn't you like to know?" the stupid body answers.

"You win," adds Cassie.

I win because I'm skinnier. I'm double zero. I stayed strong and didn't try to have my cake and eat it, too. I didn't even taste one bite.

I press my fingertips into my cheekbones. If I rammed my head into a stone wall, I bet I could fracture every bone in my face. The fingers drift over my chin, down my throat, past the butterfly wings of my thyroid, down to where my collarbones hook into my sternum like the wishbone of a bird.

Emma's cats are in the hall, scratching at the bottom of the door to get in.

My hands read a Braille map hewn from bone, starting with my hollow breasts threaded with blue-vein rivers thick with ice. I count my ribs like rosary beads, muttering incantations, fingers curling under the bony cage. They can almost touch what's hiding inside.

My skin slopes down over the empty belly, then around the inside sharp curve of my hip bones, bowls carved out of stone and painted with fading pink razor scars. I twist in the glass. My vertebrae are wet marbles piled one on top of the other. My winged shoulder blades look ready to sprout feathers.

I pick up the knife.

The tendons on the back of my hand tense, ropes holding down a tent while the wind blows. Thin scars etch the inside of my wrist, widening to the ribbons in the crook of my elbow where I cut too deep in ninth grade.

I win, I won.

I'm lost.

The music from my bedroom shrieks so loud against the mirror it's making my ears ring. I stare at the ghost-girl on the other side, her corset bones waiting to be laced even tighter so she can fold in on herself over and over until she disappears past zero.

I cut.

The first incision runs from my neck to just below my heart, deep enough so that I can finally feel something, not deep enough to flay me open. The pain flows like lava and takes my breath away.

The knife carves a path in the flesh between two ribs, then, between the two ribs below that. Fat drops of blood splash on the counter, ripe red seeds. I am so very, very strong, so iron-boned and magic that the knife draws a third line between two ribs, straight and true. Blood pools in the bowls of my hips and drips to the tile floor.

Black holes open in front of my eyes and the wild bird trapped in my heart beats her wings frantically. I'm sweating, finally warm.

The music sto—

◀ 049.00 ▶

The bathroom door swings open.

Emma sees the blood painting my skin and the red rivers carved on my body. Emma sees the wet knife, silver and bone.

The screams of my little sister shatter the mirrors.

◀ 050.00 ▶

The emergency room is filled with fog. Angry shadows fly up and down the walls and the across the ceiling.

Cassie holds my hand and whispers the numbers. "Your heart was thirty-three beats per minute in the ambulance. Wicked bradycardia. The EKG was weird, probably because of the dehydration and blood loss. You're breathing okay, but you have the blood pressure and temperature of dirt."

I close my eyes.

When they open, she has lab results.

"Anemia," she says. "Plus low blood sugar, low phosphates, low calcium, low T3—don't know what that means—high white blood cells, low platelets. They sewed you up with black thread, thirty-three stitches, isn't that weird? Oh, and you have ketones in your pee. Keep this up and we'll do New Year's together. Stay strong, sweetie."

"Where's Emma?" I ask.

A nurse drapes me in necklaces of plastic tubing and green wires, and decorates the room with plastic bags filled with water and blood. She pricks me with a needle.

I lie down in a glass-coffin dream where rosebushes climb the walls to weave me a thorny fortress.

◀ 051.00 ▶

Two days later, two days before Christmas, I am judged fat and sane enough to be kicked out of the hospital. The plan to send me straight back to New Seasons won't work. There is no room at the inn for a leather Lia-skin plumped full of messy things. Not yet. The director promises ~~Mom~~ Dr. Marrigan he'll have a bed for me next week.

I'm stable enough to go home until then. They all say I'm stable.

I failed eating, failed drinking, failed not cutting myself into shreds. Failed friendship. Failed sisterhood and daughterhood. Failed mirrors and scales and phone calls. Good thing I'm stable.

❋ ❋ ❋

Dad picks me up at the hospital. He visited every day without Jennifer (making sure he never ran into Mom) and he cried with his head on my mattress, but he hasn't said much, not even when he helped me get in the car.

It snowed while I was attached to the tubes. The white fields reflect the sun and make it almost too bright to see. I put down the visor and some girl stares back from the mirror in. Part of my brain—the hydrated, glycogen-fed part—knows that I am looking at me. But the bigger part doubts it. I don't know what I'm supposed to look like anymore. Even the name on the hospital bracelet seems weird, like the letters are in the wrong order, or part of the name is missing.

I flip the visor back up and hope Dad didn't see me wince.

The doctors tied me back together with twine. I keep forgetting about the stitches until I move too fast and the pain erupts. They pumped me full of sugar water, too, and meals served on plastic trays divided into five rectangles. This brain was on one drug and this body on another; this hand shoved food in my mouth too fast to count the bites. They tied me back together, but they didn't use double knots. My insides are draining out of the fault lines in my skin, I can feel it, but every time I check the bandages, they're dry.

I pull this self back into the body in the passenger seat of my father's car.

"Where's Emma?" I ask. "Doesn't winter break start today?"

Dad punches a button on the dashboard. The too-loud sound of a jazz trumpet crashes into us. I reach for the volume button, wince, and turn it down.

He drives for fifteen miles without saying a word.

When he gets off the highway, he does not turn right. He turns left, north, toward the dark line of storm clouds bringing more snow from the top of the world.

"Where are we going?"

"I'm taking you home."

"This isn't the way."

His fingers tighten on the steering wheel. "You're staying at your mother's until you're admitted."

"No, Daddy, please! What about Emma? She wants me to bake more gingerbread cookies with her and she needs help wrapping your presents and we're going to sing Christmas carols at church. And I promised to take her sledding and make snow angels."

He pulls into the passing lane without checking his mirrors. "You won't be seeing Emma until you're better. Maybe that will give you some incentive. If you won't try for yourself, try for her."

His voice cracks. He sniffs, swallows hard, and pushes the accelerator until the speedometer's needle rockets into the red zone. I do not know this man. I clutch the door handle, not sure if we'll make it.

✳ ✳ ✳

He still has a key to her house on the ring with the rest of them: the office, the gym, Jennifer's house, and three cars. He unlocks the door, steps in, and waits for me to follow.

~~Mom~~ Dr. Marrigan is in the library dictating notes to her computer. When we walk in, she holds up a finger so she can finish reciting details about her latest quadruple bypass on a guy who spent the last forty years eating cheeseburgers.

Dad carries my bags up to ~~the guest room~~ my bedroom. When he comes down, it looks for a minute like ~~Mom~~ Dr. Marrigan is going to tip him like a valet or a bellhop.

"Did you arrange for her ride to Dr. Parker's tomorrow?" she asks.

"Jennifer will pick her up at one and bring her back after the session." Dad zips up his jacket and pulls on his gloves. "You've taken care of the morning?"

"Why does Jennifer have to drive me?" I ask. "I can drive myself, if you let me borrow a car."

They don't even look at me. I am not in the room, apparently.

~~Mom~~ Dr. Marrigan nods at ~~Dad~~ Professor Overbrook. "One of my nurses, Melissa, will be here from the time I leave until Jennifer arrives. She can help out after Christmas, too, whenever she's not on duty. Fifteen dollars an hour, cash."

"Good," he says.

"You got me a babysitter?" I ask.

They don't react. I am still not here.

"What time will she be back?" Mom asks.

"It's a two-hour session, so with the driving, maybe four thirty, four forty-five," Dad says. "You'll be home by then, right?"

~~Mom~~ Dr. Marrigan straightens the pile of medical journals on the coffee table. "I'm on until seven. Tomorrow is Christmas Eve; Melissa is going to her brother's when Lia leaves at one. We can't ask her to come back."

He frowns. "I guess Jen could stay."

"If things are quiet, I'll sneak out early," she says.

"That would be best."

His good-bye kiss on my cheek is so light, I can't feel it. He walks out the front door and takes the time to lock it behind him.

"The blanket on the couch is plugged in and heated up," ~~Mom~~ Dr. Marrigan says. "There's a bowl of soup in there, too, beef barley. While you make that disappear, I'll explain how things are going to be."

"You're talking to me now, right?" I ask.

"I'll be there in a minute, soon as I finish this up."

After ten more minutes of dictation, she comes in and perches on the edge of the other couch, sitting as straight as if she were balancing a crown on her head. She waits for me to make the first move.

"I want to go back to Dad and Jennifer's."

She reaches to her left to click on a light. The sun sets early at the end of the year.

"We all agree you should be here," she says. "New Seasons called to confirm your intake date next week." She brushes dust off the lampshade. "They have your hospital files and will conference call with Dr. Parker after you see her tomorrow."

"I'm eighteen. What I say to her is private."

"Not if a court decides you're a danger to yourself and others."

"When did that happen?"

"I've operated on half the judges in this county, Lia. If it needs to happen, it will."

I'm not eighteen, I'm twelve, locked into toe shoes, dancing the *pas de Mom* again, with her standing in the wings, telling me what I'm doing wrong.

Steam curls off the surface of the soup. "That place didn't help me before. It's useless to send me back."

"That's what your father said."

"He did?"

"He's changed his mind about a few things, after what you did. He's finally admitting how desperate things are, but he doesn't think treatment will work."

I can't help myself. "Why not?"

"You don't want to get better. He says nothing will work until you want to be healthy and have a real life. I almost agree with him."

"So why make me go?" I ask. "Why waste the money?"

"Because if we don't, you'll die."

"You're exaggerating." I cup my hands around the soup bowl and lean into the steam, hungry now for the burning tug of the stitches. I pick up the spoon and stir. It brings up vegetables and barley from the bottom. Nanna used to make this, but I can't let me taste it. The first sip would melt through the sheet of ice that is keeping me suspended over an open hole.

I let go of the spoon and hide my hands under the blanket. "Why do you keep it so cold in here?" The words come out too loud, like my volume button is broken.

"You don't have enough body fat to maintain your temperature. The solution is to eat something nutritious every few hours. Very simple."

"I don't need to eat every few hours. I have a slow metabolism."

"Your metabolism has slowed because your body thinks you're stuck in a famine. It is holding on to every ounce it can to keep you alive."

My fists clench where she can't see them. "You're blowing my problems out of proportion so you don't have to look at why you're so miserable."

"Stop changing the subject."

"Stop bullying me. It's my life. I can do what I want."

Mom smacks her hand on the coffee table. "Not if you're killing yourself!"

The wind shrieks through French doors and blows between us, making me shiver. She stands up and paces. I fix my eyes on a faded spot of paint on the wall.

"What is the point of this irrational behavior?" she asks, her back to me. "What are you trying to prove?"

"You think I like scaring Emma and making you guys so mad you won't even look at me?"

She turns around. "I don't know. I don't understand anything you do. Drink that soup."

I pull the blanket up to my chin. "You can't force me."

She closes the heavy drapes. It cuts down on the draft and puts me in shadows. She turns on two more lights before taking a deep breath and sitting down again.

"Your body wants to live, Lia, even if your head doesn't," she says. "Your numbers rebounded quickly at the hospital; liver functions improved, QT interval improved, phosphate and calcium levels better. You're tough and I mean that in the best way possible, medically speaking."

Tough leather, stubborn stain, acid that rusts and crumbles the building.

"If you don't eat, I won't shove food down your throat, even though it's tempting. But you must stay hydrated. If you restrict fluids, you'll be placed in a psych ward. Instantly. I've already worked it out with Dr. Parker and consulted the district attorney about the paperwork."

"I will hate you forever if you throw me into a nuthouse."

"You have to take your meds, too, all of them." She picks lint off the afghan. "Melissa or I will watch you for an hour after you take them to make sure they get into your system. We'll also measure how many ounces you drink and how many you excrete."

"You're going to measure my pee?"

"It's the best way to make sure you are hydrated. There's a plastic container in the downstairs bathroom for collecting urine."

"This is ridiculous. I'm not that sick."

"The inability to rationally evaluate your situation is a result of malnourishment and disturbed brain chemistry."

"I hate it when you talk like a textbook."

She leans forward. "I hate it when you starve yourself. I hate it when you cut open your skin, and I hate it when you push us away."

The wind pushes against the glass doors so hard the drapes sway.

"I hate it, too," I whisper. "But I can't stop."

"You don't want to stop."

The poison in her voice shocks us both.

She stands again and quickly gathers up the afghan, sniffing hard and swallowing tears. At first I think she's going to walk away, maybe put the afghan in the closet or the washing machine. But she doesn't. She spreads it on top of the electric blanket that I'm hiding under, tucking it around my shoulders and hips.

"I'm sorry," she says. "That was mean."

"It was honest," I say. The weight of the blanket is sweet. "Dr. Parker would approve."

For a moment, the wind stops. The house is silent, waiting for me to tell her.

I could try. Maybe not everything. Maybe just the names, the bad names

::stupid/ugly/stupid/bitch/stupid/fat/::
::stupid/baby/stupid/stupid/stupid/stupid::

that stab me when I think about eating a cinnamon bagel or a bowl of Bluberridazzlepops. And then there is the matter of being trapped between the worlds with no compass, no map.

She smoothes my cheek with the back of her hand and leans forward but doesn't kiss me. She sniffs my head once, twice, three times.

"What are you doing?" I ask.

She sits next to me. "In med school we read about a study in which mothers could identify their babies by smell a day after they were born. I thought it was baloney."

"It's true?"

"I knew you by your smell within hours. It comforted me, like a drug, almost. I loved the smell of my daughter. I used to sniff your head all the time when you were a baby."

"Mom, that's weird. And if I think it's weird, you're really in trouble."

"I slept on your pillow for months when you moved out, pretending I could still smell you. Stupid, huh?"

I swallow hard. "Not really."

"It almost killed me when you left."

"I had to."

"I know." She looks down at her magic hands. "My only child was starving to death and I couldn't help her. What kind of mother did that make me? I was a mess." She takes a deep breath. "I wanted you here, but you didn't want to be here. I wanted you away from Cassie because she was headed for trouble. You were determined to stick with her. Cindy told me when Cassie broke off your friendship. I was so happy I almost danced in the street—"

"Do I smell like cookies?" I interrupt.

"What?"

I clear the scratchiness out of my throat. "Do I smell like cookies? My head, I mean. Like ginger and cloves and sugar?"

Her smile is warm and true. "No, not at all. I always thought you smelled like fresh strawberries. Is that weird, too?"

Neither one of us dares breathe, because we are both here in the same space and at the same time, Mommy and Lia, no phones or scalpels or burning words. Neither one of us wants to break the spell.

If I tell her about all of my ugliness now, this fragile bridge will crumble under the weight of it.

"No," I say. "It's not weird, it's sweet."

For dinner I drink electrolyte-replacement fluid that tastes like the smell of a hospital bathroom (= ? Mom took the label off and made the computer power cords disappear so I can't check the numbers). I eat a small banana (90), too. It tastes like banana.

Mom eats a chicken Caesar salad with globs of dressing and two pieces of pumpernickel bread. She watches a documentary about North Korea while I pretend to read. When it's over, she checks my stitches, pulse, and blood pressure, and gives me my meds, even my sleeping pill.

I bet she takes one, too. How else can she fall asleep without seeing all those sliced-open bodies and twitching hearts?

I fall asleep before I'm ready and wake up in the middle of the night, confused again about where I am and why and who. A thousand fingers are reaching up through my mattress, poking through my skin to scratch my bones. I leap out of the bed and pace to shake off the feeling.

Across the street at Cassie's house, a pack of wolves are digging at the rosebushes, looking for bodies to eat and bones to crunch. I can't tell anymore when I'm asleep and when I'm awake, or which is worse.

◀ 052.00 ▶

The highs and lows shifted overnight. Instead of blowing out to sea, the winter storm is stuck over the heart of New England. We're supposed to get at least two feet of snow today. I wonder if I could call someone to take Emma sledding. Mira, maybe. Or Sasha. Would they answer the phone if they knew it was me calling?

Thinking about Emma makes me want to pull out my stitches with a pair of pliers. They should burn me at the stake for what I did to her. Set me adrift on an ice floe. I wish there was a way to make her forget what she saw, to wipe that memory clean. There's not enough soap and bleach in the world.

I wouldn't have to use pliers. I could cut the stitches with nail clippers and pull until this body fell apart.

My mother calls me. I walk down the stairs.

~~The guard dog~~ Nurse Melissa arrives when we're eating breakfast (grapefruit half = 37, dry toast = 77), a giant mug of electrolyte drink (= ?) and pretty pills (= white velvet sheets wrapped around my brain). She's only a couple of years older than me but already has the don't-even-try-it forehead lines that good nurses get from constant frowning.

An hour later, I pee five hundred milliliters of yellow

water. Melissa stands in the bathroom and watches me.

"You're not getting paid enough for this," I say.

She phones in the fluid report to ~~Mom's~~ Dr. Marrigan's office.

I am dying to know how much I weigh. There are no scales here and they wouldn't tell me at the hospital. They stuck so much goo into me, I bet I put on ten pounds. My skin itches from the new fat. It's going to split and peel off me. Melissa gives me skin cream and watches while I rub it on my arms and legs.

I sleep under a mountain of blankets for the rest of the morning.

Jennifer drives me to Dr. Parker's office without saying a word. I don't blame her. I wouldn't talk to me, either, if I were her. I bet she's afraid that if she opens her mouth, she won't stop yelling at me for days and that would mess up Christmas on top of everything else.

We stay behind a plow the whole way, the wipers turned on HIGH, her hands gripped so tight on the wheel the knuckles are white. The snow makes it hard to tell up from down or see anything until we are close enough to crash into it.

She finally turns into the office park and pulls up close to the curb.

"So," I try. "Four o'clock, right?"

She nods once, eyes staring into the storm.

"And, um, I'll come over Christmas morning? So we can open presents?"

"Have your mother call me." She turns up the fan to blast the heat.

"Okay." I open the door.

"Wait." Jennifer grabs my arm. For the first time since they strapped me on the stretcher, she looks me in the eye. "David doesn't want me to say this to you, but too bad. I love you, Lia. When I married your father, I swore to love you like you were my own. But you hurt my little girl."

She is shaking with anger.

"You hurt her by starving yourself, you hurt her with your lies, and by fighting everybody who tries to help you. Emma can only sleep a couple of hours a night now. She's haunted by nightmares of monsters that eat our whole family. They eat us slowly, she says, so we can feel their sharp teeth."

My heart shifts out of idle into fourth gear, revving like a race car skidding around the track.

"I'm—"

She lets go of my arm and covers my mouth with her hand. "Shush. You go in there and you tell the truth to that woman. Tell her what's in your head and why you do these things. Tell her there is a good chance you can't live at your father's house anymore, so you better figure out how to get along with your mom."

"I can't come back?"

"I can't let you destroy Emma, too. I won't."

She turns back in her seat, suburban-stepmom mask bolted firmly in place. "Four o'clock. Maybe a little later, depending on the roads."

◀ 053.00 ▶

The receptionist, Sheila, isn't at her desk. Probably left early to cook for Christmas. I put my ear up to the closed door to Dr. Parker's inner office; someone is crying on the other side. Parker's voice murmurs, then comes the annoying *ding!* of the session timer.

I keep my eyes on the floor while the crying patient crosses through the waiting room and opens the door to the storm outside, still snuffling and hiccupping with sobs.

Dr. Parker always goes to the bathroom between sessions and sometimes takes a meditation break. It'll be at least five minutes before she calls me in. I came prepared, armed with my knitting. I need to finish this scarf/shawl/ blanket thing so I can start on something for Emma—a hat, maybe, or a sweater for her stuffed elephant.

I look out the window. A car is stuck in the parking lot. The engine races as the driver spins her tires, pushing the accelerator but going nowhere fast. Plows lumber by, chains tinkling, blades sending up sparks as they scrape the ice from the road. Everything is buried in the snow. It looks like a different world.

"Sucks, doesn't it?" Cassie says.

My heart crashbangs into my ribs.

She's sitting across the room, feet propped up on the coffee table, the magazine in her lap folded open to a crossword puzzle. She's dressed for the weather: blue coffin dress, gray ski jacket, knit cap with matching mittens on the chair next to her, damp boots lined with fur.

"They never give you a break. It's always 'talk to the shrink, talk to your mother, do what you're told, why can't you grow up?'" She fills out a couple of boxes in the puzzle, then erases them. "Thirteen down. Do you know a four-letter word for 'contract'?"

"Why won't you leave me alone?"

"I miss you."

The back of my throat tastes like I might pass out. I lean against Sheila's desk and pinch one of the cuts between my ribs. The pain lights me up like a taser. "You know what Emma saw, right?"

Cassie writes an answer in the puzzle. "'Bind,' that'll fit. Maybe."

"I can't believe I did that to her."

"You don't deserve to live." She says it like she's telling me which pair of jeans fits better. "Use a bigger knife next time. Cut deeper. Get it over with."

"I don't think I want to die."

She snorts. "Yeah, right. You can't even eat a bowl of cereal without having a meltdown. Do you honestly think you'll ever do something difficult, like, say, go to college?

Or get a job, maybe live on your own? What about shopping in the grocery store? Ooooh—scary!"

The toilet in Dr. Parker's office flushes.

I inch toward the door. "Why are you being so mean?"

"Friends tell friends the truth."

"Yeah, but not to hurt. To help."

One instant she's in the chair by the window. The next, she's standing in front of me, right up in my face, dropping the temperature below zero. Her skin is rough like a cemetery statue. Her smell is choking.

"You want me to help you, Lia-Lia?"

Can you kill a ghost by driving a knitting needle through her heart? Or least put her back in the ground where she belongs?

"Help you like you helped me?" She stretches out the last word until it rattles in her throat. "How's this then? You're not skinny. You're a pus-filled whale. Your mom wishes she had given you up for adoption. Your dad secretly thinks you're not really his kid. People laugh at you when your fat jiggles. You're ugly. You're stupid. You're boring. The only thing you're good at is starving, but you can't even do that right. You're a waste."

She winks. "And that's why I love you. Hurry up, okay?"

Dr. Parker opens the door. "Ready?"

◀ 054.00 ▸

She turns on the space heater and gives me an emergency blanket to put on top of the ugly hair afghan. "Sorry it's so cold. They really need to replace these windows."

I curl into a ball on the couch, clutching my knitting to my stomach.

She assumes her position behind the desk. "You've had a rough time of it. I'm really happy you're here. I imagine those stitches are hurting."

This is where I keep my mouth shut for fifteen minutes, pluck the white fuzz on my arms. But my heart is filled with poison and it's swelling, throwing itself against the bone cage so hard my teeth are rattling and my stitches want to pop.

"It feels like they pumped an entire ocean into me," my lips say.

"Because of the IV fluids?" she asks.

"I slosh every time I move."

"You were very dehydrated. Had you stopped drinking, too, even water?"

I take the knitting out of the bag. Knit, knit, purl. "I don't remember. Maybe."

"How are the cuts?"

"The stitches hurt more than the cuts. The doctor put in too many of them. I can hardly move without ripping them open."

She lets a quiet minute flow by, then asks, "Can I see the stitches?"

"No," I say. "Not yet."

She nods. "What else is bothering you?"

"That smell is driving me crazy." *Crap.* I wasn't going to say that.

"What smell?"

I put the needles in my lap and watch as the yarn winds itself around my hands. "You don't smell it, do you?"

She shakes her head slowly, afraid to startle this strange talking girl who is covered in my skin. "Can you describe it?"

"At first I thought it was cookies, Christmas cookies, and that I was smelling it because my stupid brain was trying to trick me into eating. But it's not that. It's Cassie. When I smell it, she's close by."

"Cassie, your friend who died last month."

"Ginger, cloves, and sugar, like burning cookies. At first it was nice. It reminded me of her. Now it scares me."

"I don't quite understand."

Oh, God. Oh, God. I am on top of the highest mountain. The icy ground is shaking, an earthquake, the world beneath me opening up with fire, steel arms ready to pull me down.

I have to move. I can't stay here anymore.

I throw myself down the mountain and open my mouth.

I tell about Nanna Marrigan's funeral and the shadows that have hovered on the edges of things ever since. I tell her about seeing ghosts in store windows and old mirrors and how most of them are quite nice, but not all.

As my lips move, the room stretches long and narrow, like the red rubber walls are being pulled by giant hands. Dr. Parker's voice shrinks as her desk moves farther and farther away from me.

"Do the ghosts frighten you?"

"Cassie does."

The yarn tightens around my hands until my fingers are purple.

"Can you tell me about that?"

I tell her. I tell her everyfreakingCassiestory, how she sat up in her coffin, how she watched me at night, how she crawled in my head, haunted every step, made it snow in the drugstore. How I stopped taking my pills, took extra pills, worked out for hours at night, stopped eating, stopped drinking, cut and cut to make her go away, to make everything go away. How nothing works. Rain, rain, rain pours down my face, nearly drowning me.

Dr. Parker keeps her tiny spider eyes locked on mine, coaxing the words out by sitting motionless in the center of her web, hardly breathing. I talk until my throat is empty and I have no feeling in my hands.

She comes out from behind the desk and gently unwinds the yarn. The blood burns back into my fingers. She wipes my tears with a soft tissue and sits next to me.

"Who else knows about this?"

"Nobody. No, wait, that's not true. Cassie knows."

"You never told your parents about seeing ghosts? Not when you were younger?"

"No way. Mom would have told me to cut the drama. Dad would have suggested I think about majoring in poetry, maybe plan on a PhD in Gothic. They never hear me; they can barely see me. I'm a doll that they've outgrown."

Dr. Parker pulls a cherry cough drop out of the pocket of her cardigan, unwraps it and puts it in her mouth. She clicks it against her teeth for a minute. Outside, the snow piles higher and higher.

Finally, she speaks. "Why are you telling me this today?"

I swallow, hard. I'm already in over my head. Might as well give her everything.

"Cassie's trying to kill me. She says I'm trapped between the living and the dead, and she wants me on her team. She's in your waiting room right now, working on a crossword puzzle."

"You saw her there?" Dr. Parker rubs the back of my hand with her fingertips.

"I told her to leave me alone. She won't."

Ding! The shut-up-now timer interrupts me.

She presses her lips together and stands, slowly, stretching the muscles in her legs and back. "Can you see Cassie now?"

"No, she's not in here, she's on the other side of that

door. Or she was. Go check the crossword puzzle. She got thirteen down wrong. She wrote 'bind.' It should have been 'oath.'"

As I explain, Dr. Parker pours water into a Styrofoam cup and sticks it in the microwave.

"You could check the magazine." I stuff my yarn into the bag. "I'm not making this up; I am not hallucinating. It's as real as the blood on my bandages, or that cough drop in your mouth."

"There is no way of proving who filled out the puzzle," she says.

"But I told you about the mistake she made."

She takes the cup out of the microwave, sticks a tea bag in it, adds a packet of sugar, and stirs it with a plastic stick. "You could have seen that when you were flipping through the pages or made the mistake yourself."

"I suppose."

There are voices in the waiting room, the next patient desperate enough to come out on Christmas Eve day in a snowstorm.

Dr. Parker hands me the cup. "Tea," she says. "Always helps."

I sip. It tastes like sweetened pencil shavings.

She sits back at her desk and picks up her pen. "I'm really proud of you, Lia. You accomplished more today than in the last two years." She makes a note on a yellow pad. "Do I have your permission to discuss this session?"

I blow my nose. "Sure, why not?"

"Thank you. I want to talk to the New Seasons director about this. We may want to develop a different treatment plan. His facility might not be the right place for you."

I blow my nose. "I can stay at home and be treated as an outpatient?"

She writes down another note before she speaks. "No. That's not what I said."

Something in her voice freezes me, my hand in the air, reaching for another tissue. "I don't get it."

"I think we should consider a psychiatric-care facility."

There is a booming noise outside, thunder in the middle of the snow. The windows shake. She keeps talking like it's an everyday thing, like she's in the habit of throwing scared little girls into nuthouses.

"You deserve the best," she continues. "Skilled people who know how to bring your mind back into balance. When the hallucinations and delusions are under control, it will be easier for you to work on your self-image issues and the relationships that cause you so much pain."

"You think I made it up," I say. "You don't believe that I see ghosts."

"I believe that you've created a metaphorical universe in which you can express your darkest fears. In one aspect, yes, I believe in ghosts, but we create them. We haunt ourselves, and sometimes we do such a good job, we lose track of reality." She stands up. "I hate to stop now, but I have another patient waiting. You really should be proud of yourself, Lia. You made a breakthrough today. How are you getting home?"

"Jennifer."

She pulls aside the curtain and looks into the parking lot. "Black SUV, right? I don't see it out there."

"She hates driving in bad weather."

"I'm sure she'll be here soon."

~~Excuse me, but did you say two minutes ago that you were recommending I go to a full-on nuthouse, for crazy people, just because I finally told you the truth?~~ "Better late than never."

I follow her to the waiting room, where a very pissed-off mom is yelling in whispers at her daughter, whose eyes look like murder. Dr. Parker waves them into her chamber.

"Take care, Lia," she tells me. "I'll call you tomorrow."

◀ 055.00 ▶

Cassie has disappeared.

I open the magazine to the crossword puzzle. Thirteen down—*bind*. Fifteen across—*Cassandra*. Seven down—*Lia*. Our names are not the answers to the clues, but they fit in the boxes.

Dr. Parker would like that. She wants me in a box the size of a diagnosis. She'll put me there so people can stare at me and stick their fingers through the bars.

※ ※ ※

I knew three girls from New Seasons who had been locked up on a psych ward: Kerry, Alvina, and Nicole. They told horror stories while we did crunches in the showers, push-ups and jumping jacks in the three A.M. moonlight. The padded walls were real, they said. And padded restraints to tie down people who went all the way over the edge. Med fogs so thick they forgot their names, screamers down the hall, lights that never turned off. It was never morning and never night, Kerry said. Never.

Would that be worse than the grown women who lived on our hall but didn't talk to us much? Wintergirls who were twenty-five, thirty, fifty-seven years old, walking around in their eleven-year-old bone cages, empty caves with bleeding eyes dragging from one treatment to the next, always being weighed, never being enough. One day the wind will carry them off. Nobody will notice.

A car rolls into the parking lot. Not Jennifer. It might be faster to walk, except I'm already half frozen and tired.

I study the diplomas on the wall. I scared Dr. Parker. She can't admit that my ghosts exist. If she did, it would destroy her version of real. If I'm right, then her ideas of trauma and behavioral modification and self-talk and closure are pretend. Fiction. Bedtime stories told to fussy patients in need of a nap.

We are both right.

The dead do walk and haunt and crawl into your bed at night. Ghosts sneak into your head when you're not looking. Stars line up and volcanoes birth out bits of glass that foretell the future. Poison berries make girls stronger, but sometimes kill them. If you howl at the moon and swear on your blood, anything you desire will be yours. Be careful what you wish for. There's always a catch.

Dr. Parker and all my parents live in a papier-mâché world. They patch up problems with strips of newspaper and a little glue.

I live in the borderlands. The word *ghost* sounds like *memory*. The word *therapy* means *exorcism*. My visions echo and multiplymultiply. I don't know how to figure out what they mean. I can't tell where they start or if they will end.

But I know this. If they shrink my head any more, or float me away on an ocean of pills, I will never return.

◀ 056.00 ▶

I dial the phone on the receptionist's desk. Jennifer's cell goes straight to voice mail. So does Daddy's. Dr. Marrigan is still at the hospital, no point even trying.

The snow is falling so fast it's hard to see the streetlights. Shadow humps of cars crawl along, small mountains on their roofs. Jennifer panics in snow, always thinks the wheels are slipping and the back end is fish-tailing. But she promised. She'll show up, drive me to my mother's house, the one without a Christmas tree because it's such a bother. I will ingest fluids and excrete them into a plastic container. Mom will make calls and take calls and do whatever she has to to keep me locked in iron dungeons.

The snow is falling fast enough to suffocate us.

I call a cab. I offer to pay double the rate because of the weather.

The guy shows up in two minutes flat. Still no Jennifer. I get in, tell him what I want. He apologizes for his heater not working. I say it doesn't matter.

The cab stops at the bank. They let me in, even though it's one minute till closing.

The cab stops at the pizza shop. They never close.

He doesn't want to drive out to the Gateway. Says there's no way he'll get a fare back into town and what happens if he gets stuck?

I wave three twenty-dollar bills in his face and ask him to hurry.

There is one car-sized hump in the motel parking lot, an El Camino. The cab driver refuses to pull in because it hasn't been plowed. I hand over his money, grab my purse, my knitting bag, and the pizza, and wade into the snow.

※ ※ ※

Elijah opens the door to Room 115, the chain still on. The wind blows off my hood. "Please."

◀ 057.00 ▶

I drag in the storm on my boots, talking desperate fast. "Okay, listen. My dad kicked me out and my mom's rules are insane."

He just stares. I shove the pizza box at him.

"Give me a 'for example,'" he says.

"She makes me pee into a plastic cup every time I go to the bathroom so she can measure it."

He puts the box on the bed. "Why?"

"She's obsessed about my body. Always has been. Made me eat tofu when I was little instead of normal baby food. She stuck me in ballet lessons when I was three. Who does that?"

"So you came here to get away for a night? A little parent-free vacation?"

I take off my mittens. "Not quite. When do you leave?"

He reaches for my mittens and carries them to the bathroom. "Tomorrow, if they clear the roads. Give me your coat. I'll hang it over the bathtub."

I unbutton the coat and take it off. "That soon?"

"Nobody reserved a room for Christmas." He carries the coat to the bathroom, grabbing a hanger as he passes the closet. "Charlie left for his sister's in Rhode Island before the storm hit. I just have to lock things up, shovel like hell, and head south."

I take a minute to breathe and look around the room. The pages and the bits of tape have been carefully peeled off the walls. The clothes from the closet and drawers have been emptied into black garbage bags by the door. The stack of notebooks is in the beat-up milk crate.

"Let me go with you." I shiver. "I just emptied my bank account. I have a lifetime of babysitting money on me, in cash. I can pay for gas and I can help drive."

"I don't know," he says. "I'm used to traveling alone."

He says more, but my ears aren't working. Blacks spots are threatening to send me to the floor. I can't pass out. This is my only option.

"I don't think you heard me," I say. "I have almost a thousand dollars and a credit card we can use until my dad cancels it. You want—"

::dizzy/gravity/floor/darkness::

◀ 058.0 ▶

I wake up in his bed. All my clothes on. Under the blankets, my feet are propped up so high on pillows, I can't see past them.

Elijah leans over me. "Are you okay? What the hell happened?"

I touch a lump on my forehead. "Must have passed out. You didn't call an ambulance, did you?"

"Should I?"

"No." I struggle to sit up.

"Are you sick?"

"A little." The black dots dance in front of my eyes again. I lay back down. "I was in the hospital for a couple days because I was dehydrated. I'm still a little wobbly, but it's not a big deal."

His eyes bug. "Are you kidding me? It's a huge deal. You can't come with me—you can't even be here. If I wind up with another dead girl, the cops won't care if I have a video alibi. You have to leave."

"I can't go home."

"I don't care where you go. You just can't stay with me."

I point out the window. "You see that storm? The police don't have enough people to handle all the accidents; half of the roads are closed because of pileups. I'm eighteen, I'm sober, I don't have any outstanding warrants. They won't come looking, I promise."

"Maybe not, but your parents will."

"They have no idea I've ever been here. I didn't tell them where you worked or how I met you."

He picks up the deck of cards on top of the television

and drops them, one by one, back onto the pile. A few slide out and land on the floor, random. "I don't have a good feeling about this."

He's going to kick me out and I'll have to call them and they'll pretend they were worried long enough to get me in a car and they'll drive me to a mental hospital where the windows are painted over and I'll never know if it's day or night and they'll keep me there until I forget my name because after that, nothing will matter.

Rain falls down my face again. "Please."

"No, don't. Don't cry. Stop. I hate it when girls cry." He goes into the bathroom and comes out with a roll of toilet paper. "Here."

I pull off a strip, wipe my eyes and blow my nose, but the tears keep leaking out.

"What happened?" He kneels by the bed so we're on the same level. "What the hell is going on?"

"I messed up," I whisper. "Big. Really big."

"Are you pregnant? Smoking crack? Robbed a bank? Shot somebody?"

"I'll show you."

I sit up again slowly, and pull off my sweatshirt, turtleneck, and long underwear shirt. As I reach for the last layer, he puts up his hands.

"No. Hold on. We're not going there. This is already not working. At all. Wait, is that blood?"

I pull off my camisole, wincing. "Help me up."

He lets me lean on his arm. I stand, counting to ten to

make sure I'm not going to pass out again, then I unwrap the bandages and let the gauze fall to the ground.

His eyes drift over the cuts and stitches, black threads poking out like broken wire. The bruises have surfaced, sunset colors stretched over the tight bones. He doesn't see my breasts or my waist or my hips. He only sees the nightmare.

"What happened?" he whispers.

"I fell off the edge of the map." I reach for the camisole and pull it back on. It is softer than the bandages. "My sister saw me do this. Her name is Emma. She's the one who plays soccer, even though she hates it. She's nine and she loves me a lot and"—I wait until my voice comes back—"and I messed her up for the rest of her life. I can't stay here. I hurt too many people."

The snow floats down, each weightless flake resting on top of another until they are heavy enough to crush in a roof.

"Can I touch your arm?" he finally asks.

"Sure."

He takes my right hand in his and pushes his thumb up the forearm along the indentation between my ulna and radius. He curls his fingers over the knob of my elbow and makes a circle with his thumb and first finger that slips easily over my bicep.

"How much do you weigh?" he asks.

"Not enough." I sniff. "Too much." A sob escapes. "I can't tell."

"Get dressed." He hands me my shirt. "You can come with me on two conditions."

"What?" I poke my head and arms through, pull the shirt down, and pick up the turtleneck.

"You have to eat enough to keep from passing out or dying."

"Fair enough."

"Second. You have to call your parents and tell them you're safe."

"No. I can't talk to them."

"If you don't call them, you can't come."

"How often do you call your family?"

His face tightens. "I don't have a family."

"You said your dad was a jerk, but you loved your mother."

"I lied. I was hatched. Raised myself."

The wind blows the storm against the motel.

"You said you weren't going to lie anymore," I say.

He looks past me at the empty walls. "You want the truth?"

"Yes."

Elijah picks up my sweatshirt, his thumb rubbing against the soft inside of the fabric. "My mother is dead. She died when I was fifteen. My father beat me for the last time a week later. He threw me out because I fought back. Best thing he ever did for me."

He hands me the sweatshirt.

"Oh," is the only thing I can say.

"I'm not bluffing," he says, stone-eyed. "If you don't call them right now, I'm on the phone with the cops and reporting you as an intruder."

I leave a message on my mother's answering machine at the house, so it will be a while before she gets it. I tell her I'm safe, I'm with a friend, and I'll call her later.

Elijah finds a Christmas movie on television. We watch it in silence. He eats a couple of slices of pizza and points at me. I eat a couple of crusts.

Two hours and two sleeping pills later, I fall asleep. No Cassie in my head. No Cassie stench in my nose. No knives, no locks, not even a single shadow in the corner. I have pizza crusts in my belly and I don't even want to stab it.

I wake up twice.

The first time the clock says 1:22 A.M. I'm dreaming about shoveling ashes. The handle of the shovel is so hot I drop it. I open my eyes. The pills made my head too heavy to lift off the pillow.

Elijah is sitting at the tiny table by the window, cigarette in his mouth, the flickering shadows from the television lighting his face. He shuffles cards once, twice, three times. Deals a hand. Puts it back in the deck and shuffles again—once, twice, three times. His sleeves are rolled up to his biceps. The man/monster tattoo on his forearm glows brighter than the end of the cigarette. Smoke rises from his skin and hangs above his head like it's on fire. Elijah becomes the monster in the skin or the monster becomes Elijah; they switch back and forth as fast as the cards being dealt on the table: *flash, flash, flash.*

My eyes fade to black.

The second time I wake up, the sun is burning through the holes in the curtains.

He's gone.

◀ 059.00 ▶

I open the curtains. The space where the El Camino was parked is partly drifted-in with snow. Looks like he got stuck twice getting out of the lot. I should have heard the spinning tires, the whining engine. I would have if I hadn't taken that second pill.

He's not really gone. He probably went to buy gas and pick up some breakfast. We should have talked about that last night. I bet I could eat a half bagel, maybe some yogurt.

I crawl back under the blankets that smell like smoke and fall asleep.

✳ ✳ ✳

One o'clock in the afternoon. It's Christmas, I think.

The plows have been by. Did he have an accident? Did he get lost?

I drink cups of hot water from the tap until my head finally clears. Two sleeping pills is definitely a mistake because it has taken me this long to realize that the milk crate with his notebooks is missing. So are his bags of pages and clothes.

But he'll come back. He has to.

At two I turn on the television and knit, back and forth, back and forth, making the half knots and twists that pull it all together on the long needles. I knit the afternoon away. I knit reasons for Elijah to come back. I knit apologies for Emma. I knit angry knots and slipped stitches for every mistake I ever made, and I knit wet, swollen stitches that look awful. I knit the sun down.

I sleep.

Wake in the dark, reach for the light, get up to pee.

When I come back, I see the piece of paper under my purse. I unfold it. There is a key inside and his note.

> *L—*
> *I know you're haunted, it's in your eyes. You have to pay attention to your visions. Deal with them.*

You can hate me for stealing your money, but not for leaving you behind. Your family wants to help. They love you.

It's not right to run from that.

Peace,

E

P.S.—The key opens the office. The vending machine is unlocked. Don't eat the cheese crackers. They're older than you are.

He left me a twenty-dollar bill. To pay for a cab, I guess.

It's snowing again. I eat two more pills and fade to white.

◀ 060.00 ▶

They say, "Eat this, Lia. Eat this please eat please just this please little bit.

"Please."

The crows stalk me, wings folded neatly behind them, hungry yellow eyes weighing my soft spots. They circle around me once, twice, three times, claws scarring the stone floor of the church.

I curl up on the frozen altar. They flutter close, black feathers filling my mouth and eyes and ears.

my body
my motel room
alone

They feed. They snatch bites with their beaks—one from my calf, one from the inside of my elbow—tug the meat from the bone and fly away with their treasure.

◀ 061.00 ▶

It takes hours to drag myself out of dream and back into the bed in room 115. No, days. Hours or days or weeks. I can't tell. I don't know how many pills I took.

Everything hurts. Worms are gnawing on my cuts, through my joints, inside my ugly bones. My heart runs rabbitfast, then lies in the mud to hibernate. If I had a knife, I'd cut deep enough to end this game. I don't even have a plastic fork.

I pick up my knitting needles.

I could.

If I really want to die, right now, this minute, in this empty place, I could stab myself in a vein; they're easy enough to see. I could walk into the blizzard and lie down in the snow and bleed out. Hypothermia and blood loss is like going to sleep, like pricking my finger on a thorn or a spindle.

I could.

A spider dangles from the lamp shade. She swings toward me, brushing over my face and landing on the headboard. She dances the thread in place and swings back. Againagainagain. Playing out thread from her tiny hands, legs slicing through the light like black knives. Her web grows, strand by strand. Each laying a path for the next step. Up-and-down threads first, then connecting them with side-to-side threads. More silk, more tension, more places to walk, weaving a world made from the inside of her.

If I had lady-spider legs, I would weave a sky where the stars lined up. Mattresses would be tied down tight to their trucks, bodies would never crash through windshields. The moon would rise above the wine-dark sea and give babies only to maidens and musicians who had prayed long and hard. Lost girls wouldn't need compasses or maps. They would find gingerbread paths to lead them out of the forest and home again.

They would never sleep in silver boxes with white velvet sheets, not until they were wrinkled-paper grandmas and ready for the trip.

The spider sighs and sings quietly to herself.

My name is Lia. My mother is Chloe, my father is David. And sister, Emma. And Jennifer.

My mother can put her hands inside the open chests of strangers and fix their broken hearts, but she doesn't know what music I like. My father thinks I am eleven. His wife keeps her promises. She brought me a sister who is waiting for me to come home and play. My name is Lia.

My bones drag out of bed, across the floor to the window. I pull the cord that opens the curtains. The sun is stuck near the ground. I don't know which way is east. I can't tell if it's twilight or dawn.

I sit back down. The mirror reflects the dim light in the window behind me, and the snow. I cannot see me in the glass. I am not there. Or here. I close my eyes, open them. It doesn't make any difference.

I turn my head at a sound—air bubbling through water. My lungs. I'm still breathing. That's a good sign.

There is a chance I might want to live, after I get some sleep.

◀ 062.00 ▶

I wake in black.

Time is stuck in molasses, blackstrap molasses poured into a mixing bowl. The mirror shows the dark outside. Night. The sun was setting, not coming up.

I am in the Gateway. 115. The monster-boy left. I pick up the phone: no dial tone. The motel is sleeping, shut down for the season.

My arms fight the blankets and my feet find the floor.

They're not waiting for me to make a decision. They're going. We're going. The cold swirls around my ankles, hungry to pull me to the ground. It takes a month to find my jacket. A year to lace up my boots.

Take knitting. Take purse. Take key.

My heart quivers, cranberry sauce dumped from a can.

Step outside.

The snow has stopped. The crescent moon hangs high, stars rubbing their hands together, teeth chattering. A glacier wind cuts into the spaces between my ribs and through the tiny cracks in my bones. I don't have much time.

I shuffle toward the office. The door to 113 is open. The lights are on.

no.

That can't be. Everything is shut down. Everything is frozen.

no.
yes.

I peek inside. Cassie is sitting cross-legged on the bed, a solitaire game spread out on the blanket. As I cross the threshold, she throws her cards in the air.

"Finally!" she shouts. "Why are you always late? You got lost again, right?"

Her room is warm. A cheap cartoon plays on the TV. There is a platter of half-eaten gingerbread cookies on the table along with a bottle of vodka. Popcorn is popping in a microwave.

She pulls me down to sit next to her. "Okay, listen. The next couple of minutes are totally going to suck. There's no way around that, sorry. I'd make it easier if I could."

"What are you talking about?"

She chuckles. "Stop kidding. This is a serious moment. You're crossing over."

"I have to call my parents."

"You can't."

"What? What is going on?"

She pats my shoulder with stone fingers. "Lia, honey? You're dying. Kind of dizzy, right? Feel wicked weird? Your heart is about to stop."

I push her hand away. "I don't want to play."

"You don't have a choice. This is your fate. It's time." She reaches for me again. Thin trails of mist flow from her fingers and twine around my arms. "Relax. It doesn't hurt that much."

"I want to go home."

"Look both ways before you cross."

"I have to teach Emma how to knit. I promised."

"They'll get her a DVD."

"But I don't want to."

She speaks slowly. "Your kidneys failed a couple hours ago. Starvation plus dehydration plus exhaustion topped off with an almost-overdose? Nice job, Lia-Lia. Nice job, indeed. Your lungs are filling. Just a few more minutes. Relax."

She leans forward and exhales a wreath of mist that falls over me like bonfire smoke. My heart flops once. I try to breathe. My lungs don't expand.

For a moment, one glass-coffin moment, I want to give in. Freeze. Bleed out. Surrender would be easy to swallow. I could sleep forever after.

My stupid heart flops again in the mud, not ready to hibernate yet. One more time, and then a third beat, faster. It kindles a tiny fire in my blood.

I wave my arms to break through the mist. "Open your mouth."

"Huh?"

"If I'm dying, you have to be nice to me. Come on, Cass, one little favor."

She shrugs and sighs, then opens up. On her tongue lies the green disk, see-glass born inside a volcano and buried with her in the ground. I snatch it.

"No!" she shrieks.

I try to get up, but my legs aren't listening.

"It's mine!" She slaps my arm.

The glass flies through the air and bounces on the carpet. We scramble over each other, body and shadow, bone and shimmer. She lands closest, but she doesn't see it. I reach under the side table, pretending it's there. She grabs the back of my jacket and heaves me to the side.

"Ha," she mutters, groping under the table.

I tip-tip my fingers through the carpet until they find it. Her head is halfway under the table. I hold the glass to my eye.

It's filthy.

I lick it, green lollipop sizzle on my tongue. The noise makes Cassie freeze. She turns around as I hold it up again and look through the leaf-colored crystal out the window to the stars lining up above us.

Her scream is wrapped in white velvet, elegant and muffled.

The light beyond my eyes flashflashflashes with a hundred futures for me. Doctor. Ship's captain. Forest ranger. Librarian. Beloved of that man or that woman or those children or those people who voted for me or who painted my picture. Poet. Acrobat. Engineer. Friend. Guardian. Avenging whirlwind. A million futures—not all pretty, not all long, but all of them mine.

"You lied!" I say. "I do have a choice."

Cassie flops back on the bed, pouting, arms crossed over her chest. "That's right. Leave me alone. Go have a real life. My bad for screwing up."

I hold out the glass. "Look through this. Maybe you can come back."

"It doesn't work that way. There are some laws in physics that are real, you know. I can't change them. I'm stuck here forever."

"Stuck in the middle? In between worlds?"

"Yeah, that's the classic definition of a ghost, isn't it?"

"Do you want to be all the way dead?" I ask.

"Yes." She shakes her head, ignoring the tears in her eyes. "No. Maybe. I get glimpses of it sometimes, like a countryside that you can see from an airplane. Something about it reminds me of being a kid, when the world was our kingdom, but I don't know why."

My heart is waving a red flag. I have to hurry.

"Quick," I say. "Tell me what you miss the most."

"What?"

"What do you miss about being alive?"

Her eyes blur with summer clouds. "The sound of my mom singing, a little off-key. The way my dad went to all my swim meets and I could hear his whistle when my head was underwater, even if he did yell at me afterward for not trying harder."

While she talks, I move slowly to the door. She doesn't notice.

"I miss going to the library. I miss the smell of clothes fresh out of the dryer. I miss diving off the highest board and nailing the landing. I miss waffles. Oh." Her head tilts back, like she's high on a swing. Her edges are fading. "Oh, this is awesome, Lia. I never thought of trying this, of taking the best parts with me."

I open the door. "Do you feel better?"

She's transparent. "Best."

"Good." My heart lurches.

"Go to the office," she says, her body disappearing like a mist in the sun. "The pay phone on the wall still works. There are quarters in the top drawer. Hurry."

"I'm sorry," I say. "Sorry I didn't answer."

Her eyes glitter like stars. "I'm sorry I didn't call sooner."

◀ 063.00 ▶

It takes almost the rest of my life to get to the office but because the moon is paying attention to my visions and the stars are lined up, the quarters are in the drawer and the pay phone does work.

I call my mother and give her directions so she can find me. I tell her that I'm finally alive, but that she should hurry.

The paramedics zap my heart with their magic wands as we speed to the hospital. Once, twice, three times.

◀ 064.00 ▶

They tell me I was ten days in the hospital.
   I slept. Dreamless.

◀ 065.00 ▶

My third visit to New Seasons is the longest one yet, a
marathon, not a sprint to the exit. I walk, mostly. Stop
and sit down when I'm tired. Ask a lot of questions. Every
once in a while I spend a day or three with storm clouds in
my head. I sit some more, quiet, until they pass.

   No games this time. No midnight exercise parties in
the shower for me. No dumping my food in the plants or
sticking it in my underwear or bribing an attendant to lie
about my intake. I avoid the drama of the girls still neck-
deep in the snow, running away from the pain as fast as
they can. I hope they figure it out.

   The concept of eating is scary. The nasty voices are
always on call, eager to pull me back down

      ::Stupid/ugly/stupid/bitch/stupid/fat/
      stupid/baby/stupid/loser/stupid/lost::

but I do not let them. I put all of the bites in my mouth and
try not to count. It's hard. I take half a cinnamon bagel

and the numbers jump out at me, *boo!* Half a bagel (165). Whole bagel (330). Two tablespoons full-fat cream cheese (80).

I breathe in slowly. *Food is life.* I exhale, take another breath. *Food is life.* And that's the problem. When you're alive, people can hurt you. It's easier to crawl into a bone cage or a snowdrift of confusion. It's easier to lock everybody out.

But it's a lie.

Food is life. I reach for the second half of the bagel and spread cream cheese on both. I have no idea how much I weigh. This scares me almost to death, but I'm working on it. I am beginning to measure myself in strength, not pounds. Sometimes in smiles.

I read a lot. Emerson, Thoreau, Watts. Sonya Sanchez; he was right, she's amazing. The Bible, a couple of pages. The Bhagavad Gita, Dr. Seuss, Santayana. I write awkward, random poetry. Our floor goes on a field trip to a restaurant. I eat a waffle with syrup and I ask for more.

They're teaching me how to play bridge. I'm not interested in poker. All bets are off.

Mom and Dad and Jennifer visit. We talk and talk until the dams burst and the tears flow with a little blood, because we're all angry. But nobody storms out of our sessions. Nobody uses nasty names. We take turns shoveling through years of muck. Sometimes I think my skin will burst into flames. I'm angry at them. I'm angry at us. I'm angry that I starved my brain and that I sat shivering in my bed at night instead of dancing or reading poetry or eating ice cream or kissing a boy or maybe a girl with gentle lips and strong hands.

I'm learning how to be angry and sad and lonely and joyful and excited and afraid and happy. I am learning how to taste everything.

I don't lie to the nurses this time. I don't argue with them or throw anything or scream. I argue with the doctors because I don't believe in their brand of magic, not a hundred percent, and it's something I need to talk about. They listen. Take notes. Suggest that I write down what it looks like to me. At least they don't think I'm crazy because I see ghosts.

My brain stirs and yawns when they take away the crazy candies. It grows when I feed it.

Another page turns on the calendar, April now, not March. Dr. Parker visits. She and the inpatient team are putting together a transition plan for me so I can shift from hospital Lia to real Lia.

"Who cares if we call it a depression or a haunting?" she asks. "You haven't cut yourself since you got here. You're talking. You're eating. You're blooming. That's all that matters."

❋ ❋ ❋

Cassie's parents show up the day the crocuses open. We cry.

I miss Cassie so much I can only think about her in sad, short gasps. She shows up now and then but rarely says anything. Mostly, she watches me knit. I'm making my mom a sweater.

I write Emma a letter every single day. When they finally let her come, she brings me a get-well card signed by her whole class. Her cast is off, but she doesn't want to play softball. Lacrosse is the cool sport this year.

Her hug makes me strong enough to carry the entire world on my shoulders. She wants me to come home soon. I'm almost ready.

I am spinning the silk threads of my story, weaving the fabric of my world. The tiny elf dancer became a wooden doll whose strings were jerked by people not paying attention. I spun out of control. Eating was hard. Breathing was hard. Living was hardest.

I wanted to swallow the bitter seeds of forgetfulness.

Cassie did, too. We leaned on each other, lost in the dark and wandering in endless circles. She got too tired and went to sleep. Somehow, I dragged myself out of the dark and asked for help.

I spin and weave and knit my words and visions until a life starts to take shape.

There is no magic cure, no making it all go away forever. There are only small steps upward; an easier day, an unexpected laugh, a mirror that doesn't matter anymore.

I am thawing.

◄ Acknowledgments ►

I journeyed into the land of the Wintergirls because of the countless readers who wrote and talked to me about their struggles with eating disorders, cutting, and feeling lost. Their courage and honesty put me on the path to find Lia and helped me understand her brokenness. While Lia's story is not based on any living person, it was inspired by those readers and I thank them.

Dr. Susan J. Kressly, of Doylestown, Pennsylvania, is an extraordinary pediatrician, a wonderful stepmother to my daughters, and a very good friend. Sue nudged me for years to tackle the topic of eating disorders and provided me with valuable feedback on early drafts of the manuscript. I appreciate both the nudging and the help. This book would not have been written without her.

Psychotherapist Gail Simon has specialized in treating patients with eating disorders in Buckingham, Pennsylvania, for twenty-three years, in addition to working at a residential treatment center for eating disorders for almost two decades. Gail graciously read the manuscript to make sure that Lia's physical and psychological deterioration were accurately described. I am very grateful for her assistance.

It takes a village to raise a book, too. My village sits in the tall building in lower Manhattan that contains the offices of Penguin Books. I am a very fortunate author to be working with the brilliant editor Joy Peskin. Her gentle questions and keen eye helped bring Lia's story into sharper focus for me, and her moral support helped guide me out of the storms of self-doubt. Many thanks also to Regina Hayes, president and publisher of the Viking division of Penguin, who is a hero to me in more ways than I can count. Copy editor Susan Casel saved me from public semicolon embarrassment. I thank her for not having a meltdown over the stylistic quirks of the text. Thanks to proofreader Shelly Perron and executive production editor Janet Pascal for helping my text walk the straight and narrow rules of grammar and consistency.

The Penguin design team of Linda McCarthy, Natalie Sousa, Dani Delaney, and Nancy Brennan get all of the credit and deep gratitude from me for creating this beautiful book. The cover image is a photograph taken by the young and extremely talented Alexandre Denomay of Montreal, Canada. I thank him for sharing his gifts with my story.

Greg Anderson, my first husband (now married to Dr. Sue, see above) and still my friend, usually helps me out by going over my manuscript for grammar mistakes. He didn't get a chance to do that with *Wintergirls*, and I promised him I would mention this. If you do find a grammar mistake, please know that it's not Greg's fault.

My early readers, Genevieve Gagne-Hawes, my daughters Stephanie and Meredith Anderson, Allison Sands, and Maria Grammer all offered valuable suggestions and support. Meredith and Allison in particular responded to the story in a way that is every author's dream. Thank you also to my children Jessica and Christian Larrabee for lots of encouragement and for keeping the music turned down when I was trying to untangle plot threads.

Writing books like this often takes an author to that liminal place between reality and imagination. That's why we need practical people who are firmly grounded in the real world. Thank you Amy Berkower, and everyone at Writers House, for keeping track of the details and allowing me to wander in the forests of my mind. I am a fortunate author indeed, for Amy is a much-appreciated friend as well as my agent.

This book would not have been written without the strength and love of my husband, Scot. I do not have the words to explain how important his presence is to my writing. I trust that he can see the depth of my gratitude when he looks in my eyes.

And finally, a long overdue recognition.

I was granted a scholarship to Manlius Pebble Hill School in Dewitt, New York, when I was in eighth grade. I am not sure why they gave it to me. I was an underwhelming student who spent most of her time daydreaming in the back row. Somebody, somewhere, must have seen potential in me, but it could have been a clerical error. Whatever the cause, I was given significant tuition assistance and spent the most important year of my education at that fine school.

My English teacher at MPH was an elderly gentleman named David Edwards. He was near retirement after a long career spent largely teaching boys in a military academy. A more unlikely teacher-student combination cannot be imagined. Mr. Edwards taught me Greek mythology, old-school style. He filled my head with the stories of gods, mortals, magic, and transformation that laid the foundation for my writing life. I am sorry that he died before I could give him one of my books.

I suspect that I frustrated Mr. Edwards, because he didn't think I was paying attention in class. But I was. I am forever in his debt for teaching me.